Simon led Catherine through the steps of the waltz. She followed him easily, for there was a splendor flowing with the gentle call of the music. Or was it being in his arms that made her heart feel like singing while her feet seemed to fly? His hand on her back was magic, lighting a fire in her soul, its warmth spreading out to her fingers and toes and stealing her breath at the same time.

"You're a fast learner," Simon said quietly.

"Oh, no." She was quick to disclaim all credit. "It is because you are so good at leading."

Simon's hold on her tightened. Or was it just his hold on her heart? "Perhaps we are well matched," he said under his breath.

"Perhaps." But she liked that idea and held it closely to her as they moved to the music. Might she dare to hope that what began as a desperate grab for safety on her part was turning into something real?

Hearts in Hiding
Anne Hillary

PINNACLE BOOKS
WINDSOR PUBLISHING CORP.

PINNACLE BOOKS

are published by

Windsor Publishing Corp.
475 Park Avenue South
New York, NY 10016

First Printing: February, 1991

Printed in the United States of America

Prologue

November 1813

Light snow danced on Simon Bradford's face and brought him back to restless consciousness. Its gentle touch was so at odds with the misery and stench around him that it penetrated his pain-filled nightmares and gave him the strength to open his eyes. The demons of his sleep were still around him though. There was no escape.

How many days was it since the battle? he wondered. He remembered the long march from Montreal to Chrysler's Farm—ninety miles, Colonel Morrison had said, but in the freezing rains of late fall it had seemed at least half the distance back home to London. There had been about eight hundred of them, a small band compared to the Americans, but somehow they had been the victors. Or at least they had won the battle, but since his men had led the attack and led the casualties, too, most likely, had they really won? Who else had been wounded? Who had died? Days and nights had swirled together into a whirlpool of confusion. He had lain on this farm cart forever, its uneven progress reminding him that the pain could get worse and would as soon as they jarred in and out of the next frozen rut.

Slowly he turned his head. He wasn't the only one on the wagon; another man lay next to him, his face gripped with agony. The snowflakes falling on the bloodied rag around his head turned red while his beard grew whiter by the moment.

The cart hit another bump and from the moans of pain, Simon knew that the wagon was crowded with the wounded, the leavings of a battle that wouldn't even slow the planning of the holiday parties back home. While men were dying all around him, couples would be dancing before the yule log and gentlemen would be gambling at Brooks. But Madeline would know. Two people as bound with love as they were knew when harm befell the other. She would know as surely as if she were right there with him.

He closed his eyes again, his spirit calling to her. Her hands would be gentle and healing. Their touch would bring no pain, only comfort, and under her ministerings he would be whole again. He saw her eyes, so blue that even the sky seemed to be only a faded echo of their beauty. How they could glow with love!

He sighed and moved restlessly; the pain that had driven him into a deep nightmarish sleep now kept him from any kind of rest. The bitter cold had numbed his hands and feet, the blood on his clothes had frozen into stiff slabs of ice that gave him no protection from the storm that raced with them back to Montreal. Yet, in spite of the freezing winds, the wounds in his arm and leg burned with a fire that surely must consume him and left his face covered with sweat.

What had he been thinking of, to wish Madeline here? What kind of love did he have for her that would bring her to this horrible place, to witness all this wretched misery? She was a lady, a delicate creature pampered by love. She was to be comforted and protected, her beautiful hands were meant for gathering roses and plucking at the harp; to stain them with blood would be a desecration.

The rest of the journey passed in a bloodred haze. Bandages were changed and the wounded were fed, but they were ever hurrying forward. To linger, trying for a gentler road, would only bring more death.

Late one afternoon they reached the old church that had been turned into an army hospital. The pews had been removed and pallets put in their place, but there was no way to make the building light. The high windows were stained glass, dark and moody, and the ones that were broken were merely boarded over. It smelled more of death than life to Simon, yet at least it was out of the bitter wind.

He was tended to quickly after his arrival, but he didn't know if it was in deference to his rank of major or the seriousness of his condition. They cleaned and rebandaged the saber wound in his arm and removed the pellets from his leg. The doctor's face was grim as he worked, and Simon didn't have the heart to ask for his prognosis. He would make it. He had to. Madeline was waiting for him.

The days dissolved into weeks as fevers and chills claimed his body. The saber wound healed, but those in his leg wouldn't. He lay half awake long hours, staring up into the vaulted arches of the old church, wondering what spirits were lurking high above, and what they thought of the pain below.

There was no way that the hospital could be kept warm. The raging Canadian winds had rattled the boards covering the windows and pounded at the doors, mocking any attempt to keep out the cold. There were thousands of little cracks that the wind found to slip in and steal any warmth the feeble fires were giving. The doctors and their helpers wore heavy coats all day long, rarely even taking off their woolen gloves when examining him. Water and blood that spilled on the floor froze, and snow collected in the niches that housed the church's statues, who gazed serenely down on the suffering.

During his first weeks at that hospital Simon was aware only of the pain and the cold. While the cold brought a numbing relief to his body, he instinctively preferred the pain, for it meant he was still alive.

"We'll have to operate," Dr. Farwell told him one day after the pain had become unbearable.

Simon didn't ask what he was going to do. He knew that operations were the last attempt, what they tried on a patient who was sure to die anyway. He whispered his consent.

Dr. Farwell wasted no time, immediately ordering

8

two soldiers to carry Simon's cot into the sacristy. The vestments and candlesticks had been replaced with medical equipment, and a small stove in the corner made the room unbearably hot.

The soldiers lifted Simon onto a large table in the center of the room. Several oil lamps hung around him, giving the room an unnatural glow and staining the ceiling with a smoky film.

Dr. Farwell took off his coat and his woolen gloves, and examined a selection of evil-looking blades. Simon watched with little interest.

"Pour him out a stiff measure," the doctor ordered.

A soldier reached for a half-empty bottle of brandy and filled a glass with liquor. Then he carried it over to Simon, the brandy slopping down the sides of the glass and onto the floor.

" 'Ere you go, mate," the soldier said briskly. "This 'ere's the best the doc serves. Ya won't feel a thing." With one big hand he raised Simon's shoulders and held the glass to his lips.

Simon knew that drink was the best way to survive the pain of an operation, but the fiery liquid was too much for him in his weakened state. He choked and gasped for breath.

The doctor waved the brandy away and moved his instruments closer. Two soldiers came and held Simon down, but the doctor's first touch caused Simon to cry out in pain and he lost consciousness.

It was then that Madeline came to him. He heard her voice and felt her soothing hands. Her love made her strong enough for both of them, and suddenly he was well. Together they ran laughing

9

through fields of wildflowers and sunshine. She fell into his arms, her eyes alight with love and wanting, and he drank deeply of the magic of her touch. Her laughter caressed him, and he needed her with a hunger unknown to him. Nothing could keep him from her and nothing, no one, would stand between them ever again.

When he awoke, Simon was back in the wretched hospital, his own body paining and aching. No one else had seen Madeline, but he knew that she had been there. Her love had healed him and made him live. Soon he would be strong enough to go home. Home to England and to his Madeline.

Chapter One

March 1814

The sun broke through the clouds with an unexpected burst of brilliance that danced flashes of light across the waves. The *Flying Arrow* took heart from the appearance of the sun and strained forward, living up to its name. The wind filled the stiff canvas sails, and the ship slid forward through the restless waters.

Simon Bradford leaned against the port gangway and stared out over the water. It was two days since they had left Halifax, and this was the first real wind they had encountered. Even though it stirred the waves into a wild frenzy that pitched the boat about, it was good to be moving toward home. Lord! It had been a long three years!

He moved away from the side of the ship and walked stiffly along the deck. An old sailor walked by him.

"Major," he nodded quietly.

Simon nodded back and reached out to steady himself on one of the great guns that lined each side of the ship. Although this was not an actual warship, it was prepared to defend itself against any American vessels that it might meet, but Simon fervently hoped that that would be unnecessary as he grimaced down at the cane he was forced to use. He had had quite enough of fighting and killing to last a lifetime, and wanted only to forget the battles he had been in.

Unfortunately, his leg was not ready to let him forget. He had thought it was healing rather well until he had come on board. Though he could walk passably on land, the movement of the sea made it almost impossible to walk without pain. How could he present himself to Madeline in such a condition?

Madeline. Madeline. Simon smiled at the sound of her name. He reached the main mast in his walk around the deck and held on to the belaying pins for support. He put his head back, watching the clouds racing across the sky.

The last time he had seen Madeline, she had been wearing a dress of that same blue as the sky. The wind had blown her dark hair out of its pins and she had had to put up one hand to keep her hair from blowing in her face. Her deep blue eyes had filled with tears as she had strained against her father's arm, wanting to run to Simon, but her father's hold had been tight, and the only memories Simon had taken with him were of quick, stolen kisses, and the all-too-brief moments he had held her in his arms.

She had been only sixteen to his twenty-five

years. Her father had insisted that she was too young and that Simon had not proved himself worthy of her.

Damn! Her father had been a proud one. He had ranked himself and his family among the most elite of society and disliked them to associate with anyone he deemed inferior. All were judged by their titles, or lack thereof, and their social connections.

Would he be considered worthy now? Simon wondered. He had distinguished himself in battle and had gained the respect of his superiors and the men he had commanded. Would any of that count with Madeline's father? Not that it mattered. He would find that Simon was no longer the inexperienced greenhorn he had been. He had learned how to fight for what was rightfully his, and fight was exactly what he would do to keep Madeline.

Somewhere deep in the bowels of the ship a bell tolled and Simon pulled a watch from his waistcoat pocket. He had only a short time to change before dinner. He turned around and slowly made his way down several flights of stairs to his cabin. Every day brought him closer and closer to Madeline, yet he chafed at the slow passage of time. He needed her now, and found patience only in the fact that his leg needed more time to heal.

By the time he reached his cabin, Simon was worn out by the exertion of his walk. He sank down onto the bottom bunk, gingerly raising his leg up so that it also rested on the bed. He closed his eyes in relief as the ache subsided.

His eyes popped open again though, his peace too short-lived for his liking. He could have sworn he heard a baby crying! That was ridiculous, he chided himself, and forced himself to relax. No one would bring a baby on a journey such as this, especially not during wartime.

The sounds came again, clearly close by, and Simon rose to his feet. It was most likely some half-witted sailor's idea of a joke, but Simon would disabuse him of that notion. He picked up his cane and limped toward the door. The crying was even louder in the hallway and seemed to be coming from the cabin just across the hall from his. He went forward and rapped sharply on the door, intending to give the prankster a piece of his mind.

The door swung open and a young girl stood in the opening, turned away from him as she reached for something. Clad in a worn black dress of little distinction, her slender body proclaimed her youth and inexperience. A squawling baby was perched on her hip.

"It's about time you came back," she said as she swung around to face him. A pail was clutched in her hand, but she stopped seeing Simon before her. "You're not the cabin boy."

"No," Simon said. He tried to keep the impatience, the weariness from his voice but wasn't sure how successful he'd been.

The girl seemed not to notice though as the baby began to fuss again. She shoved the bucket into Simon's hands and tried to soothe the infant's screams, rocking him gently and making soft cooing noises, but the baby refused to quiet.

"Oh, Teddy, do stop," she pleaded, sounding close to tears herself.

It was obvious to Simon that the girl was not capable of caring for the infant, and he looked past her into the cabin. It was as small as his own, but there was no sign of the girl's mistress.

"Perhaps I could get your mistress for you." He was no longer angry, yet still desirous of quiet.

"My what?" The girl stared up at him. She was very pale, and dark circles of weariness made her brilliant blue eyes seem huge. Perspiration dotted her forehead and dampened the curls that framed it. She pushed a few strands of hair from her face with a hand that was so thin it was almost frail.

"Your mistress," he repeated. "Whoever left you with the baby. I certainly don't want to cause you trouble, but isn't there someone who can keep him quiet?"

A worried look pulled at her lips, and she suddenly noticed that he still held the bucket in his hands. She quickly took it away from him and put it down near the doorway.

"I'm sorry if Teddy's disturbed you," she apologized. "He's normally such a good baby. He slept all day yesterday and I thought maybe the movement of the water relaxed him, but he's been so fretful today. . . ."

Simon frowned at the girl. She had a certain air about her, and her manner of speech seemed to indicate a well-bred young lady. Yet, her clothing was of coarse material and her hands were red and raw from work.

A cabin boy went down the passageway behind Simon. "Oh, here," she called. As she grabbed the bucket and leaned out the door, Simon saw the glint of a ring on her hand.

"Oh, Tom."

The boy stopped walking but looked anything but eager to help. "I ain't no lady's maid," he grumbled. "Ya shoulda brought one with you if you wanted ta be waited on."

Simon's anger burst alive again, fueled by the boy's insolence and his own embarrassment. His steps were sure for once as he grabbed the boy quickly by the front of his shirt and dragged him closer. "I believe the lady was in need of your assistance."

The boy nodded with sudden respect and took the bucket, practically running down the hall with it.

"I must thank you," the girl said with a laugh. "That's the fastest I've ever seen him move."

Her soft and gentle smile only increased Simon's discomfiture. "No, it is I who must offer my apologies," he said stiffly. "I hope I did not offend you by my presumption of your position."

She laughed again, the exhaustion and worry leaving her face for a moment, and Simon caught a glimpse of a young woman, fresh and lovely as springtime. Something warmed in his soul. "I was not offended. After all, how were you to know that I was not an inefficient nursery maid, but an ineffectual mother?"

Some of the worry crept back into her face as she stared down at the restless infant in her arms. He was no longer crying, but whining softly. Simon shifted his weight uneasily under the sight of her burdens. He wished the carefree young woman of the laughter would return to replace this woman bent under worries too great for her.

"Shall I find your husband for you?" he offered. She did not look old enough to be married or have a child, but she was wearing a wedding ring. "At least, he could fetch Tom to run errands."

Her head bowed, the girl continued to watch the child for a long moment. When she finally glanced back up at him, her eyes were old and tired, her full lips pulled and weary. "My husband died several months ago." Her quiet voice was twisted with pain.

Simon silently cursed his clumsiness. "I am very sorry," he murmured. "I only hope that my questions have not increased your burden."

Surprisingly, she laughed again, the sound richer and fuller for the pain it tried to hide. "My position is sufficiently insecure that I need no one's questions to remind me of it. And you were only trying to help, so please put it out of your mind."

He relaxed slightly. He had no choice but to do so, for her kind manner forbade him to remain embarrassed. Yet it was more than that. He was impressed by her thoughtfulness and wanted to be of service. "Are there no other women on board who might help you? Surely on a ship this size . . ."

The woman shook her head. "Not many women wish to travel during wartime, only those who have no choice. I fear the only other women here are an elderly lady and her companion." She tried to smile, but it was a weak attempt. "And they were rather censorious of me for traveling alone, so I do not think they would be likely to help me with

Teddy."

The ship shuddered and both Simon and the girl lost their balance. He steadied himself against the doorway, and reached out to keep her from falling. Her skin was smooth as a baby's, yet very much a woman's.

"Perhaps you should sit down," he said to her.

She nodded and sank to the edge of the bed. Teddy continued to fuss in spite of her efforts to soothe him.

Simon watched them for a moment, not certain what good he could do if he stayed, but not willing to leave yet either. There was something about the woman that drew him, her obvious need, he guessed, though something in his heart kept him from exploring that thought much further. Instead, he crossed the room, sitting down on a narrow bench bolted to the ship's wall and staring at the baby in the woman's arms. He wanted to help her, she was so alone and obviously in need of comfort, yet he knew nothing about babies. "Perhaps he is seasick," he suggested.

"Can babies get seasick?"

Simon could only shrug. Wrapped in such warm and loving arms, any infant should be content. Since Teddy wasn't, he had to be hungry, wet, or sick. Surely she would have checked for the first two. "Is there a doctor on board?"

She shook her head. "Only an old sailor who does what doctoring's needed aboard the ship, but he knows far more about gunshot wounds than about babies."

Simon's lips tightened. That was more in his line

18

also, yet he had been trying to forget it. The girl must have noticed his discomfort, for her eyes seemed to linger suddenly on his cane. She blushed and quickly turned away as Tom came back with a bucket of water.

"Just put it inside the door," she called to the boy. He did as she instructed and hurried away. She turned to Simon. "I was afraid he was slightly feverish, and thought perhaps if I bathed him . . ."

Simon stood up, uncomfortably aware of the awkwardness of his movements now where he hadn't been just a moment before. Even the cabin boy, awkward and surly as he was, moved with more surity than Simon did. He bowed slightly toward the woman. "If there is anything I can do to help you, please let me know."

She smiled her gratitude. "It's enough to know that there is a friendly face on board. But if you happen to see Tom, would you ask him to bring my dinner here?"

Simon nodded and walked toward the door. He tried not to wince as the movement of the boat caused him to put his weight unexpectedly on his weaker leg. The thought that she might pity him sickened him, and seemed to make his gait more unsteady. She was the one that needed help, not him. "It will be my pleasure, Mrs. . . ."

"Mrs. Smith. Catherine Smith," she said quickly. "And this is Teddy."

Simon held on to the door, bowing in acknowledgment. "And I am Simon Bradford." He hoped that she had not noticed how tightly he had had to grasp the door for support as he closed it

19

behind him.

The wind was still strong the next day, although the sea seemed less rough. Yet they were being pushed closer to home, so Simon curbed his restless impatience. After a light luncheon he climbed to the deck again and began his laborious stroll around the deck. Pain shot through his leg, but he forced himself to keep going. Exercise was what he needed, for he could not face Madeline as a cripple.

With the wind at his back, pushing him and the ship ever closer to his love, Simon felt his excitement grow. Soon they would be together, soon his happiness would be complete. Life could hold no more joy than when he would hold Madeline in his arms. The ship, the racing clouds, disappeared, and Madeline was dancing before him, her eyes sparkling with love and promise. The pain in his leg was a dull, barely noticed ache.

Suddenly the dream faded as Simon became aware of someone next to him. He turned to see Mrs. Smith. Out in the warm sunshine she seemed even smaller than he had remembered, her plain gray dress only emphasizing her slight figure. She did not seem demure and self-effacing, though, for her eyes were alive with curiosity and excitement as she looked around her. He could not help but smile; her interest and enjoyment were contagious.

"I can see in your eyes that Teddy must be better."

"Yes, he is sleeping, but you needn't pretend that his crying did not keep you awake most of the night."

"Actually, I slept well, but I don't think we can say the same for you." The lines of worry might have faded, but the clear light of the sun showed that she was still pale and exhausted. His heart twisted in sympathy for her. "Perhaps you should be below decks also, taking advantage of his silence to rest yourself."

She lifted her face to the wind and shook her head softly. The wind blew through her light brown hair as she smiled at him. The breeze seemed to have blown a freedom into her eyes. "I had planned to, but I needed to see the sky more than I needed sleep. All too soon Teddy will be awake and I shall be imprisoned in that stuffy little cabin again." Her laughter took away any resentment her words might have indicated, and her voice was soft with love for her son. "Might I take a turn around the deck with you?"

"I should be honored." Simon bowed. He enjoyed her cheerful enthusiasm, but his gait, unnoticed amid his dreams of Madeline, now seemed uneven and awkward. Mrs. Smith appeared not to notice.

"Isn't it strange how life arranges things?" she mused, as if they were strolling through Regent's Park, not across the weatherworn planking of a ship's deck. "My father had always wanted me to go to England someday, but I'm certain he had not ever thought it would be with a three-month-old infant and wearing widow's weeds."

"Your father was from England?"

She turned toward him to nod. "Yes, but it had been more than twenty years since he left. He built

21

a prosperous business in Boston, but after my mother died and the trouble between England and the States became worse, we moved to Halifax."

"And was it there that you met Mr. Smith?"

"Lieutenant Smith," she corrected Simon absently. "Yes, he and my father were great friends. Not long after we were married, my father died." Her voice quivered slightly as the memories shifted from pleasant to painful. Her tone grew soft, thoughtful. "I think now, my father must have known he was ill, and wanted to see me taken care of before he died. Except that I doubt he expected me to be burying my husband only a month after him."

Simon was silent for a moment as they reached the bow of the ship and turned back. His tiresome leg seemed a small problem compared to those she had. "Did the lieutenant die before his son was born?"

She nodded, then spoke. "So Teddy and I are alone." Her voice was crisp and businesslike, devoid of all emotion. "Except for my husband's family in England, and I can't say that I'm too eager to meet them. I did write after my husband died, but I never heard from them. The mails are so unpredictable with the war on though, so they may never have received the letter. After Teddy was born I was going to write again, but it seemed so silly. I had no choice but to go to them, and I could arrive as quickly as my letter. Looking back, I wonder if I acted too rashly. Perhaps they will not welcome us into their family, yet I will have forced myself upon them." Her nervous laugh betrayed her fears.

"I cannot conceive of any family that would not welcome you into their midst," Simon said.

She did not smile or murmur her thanks, but frowned up at him. "Are you all right? You appear dreadfully pale."

He tried to shrug off her question, even though the aching in his leg had grown into pain, causing beads of sweat to form on his upper lip. "No, no, it is nothing. Just an old wound that is acting up slightly."

Mrs. Smith stopped walking and looked at him suspiciously. "Just how old is this old wound?" She sounded much more like Teddy's mother, or any mother, actually.

"About four months."

"Four months! Why aren't you resting instead of stomping about up here?"

Her obvious concern touched him, and he smiled at her. "It was not all that serious. In fact, I barely noticed it while I was on land. It just seems weaker because of the unsteadiness of the ship."

"Then you should not be walking on it."

"Oh, no." Simon shook his head and began walking again. The exercise was what he needed to become worthy of Madeline again, he told himself, but he also was walking to escape the compassion in her eyes. "I must use this time to make my leg strong," he told her. "I cannot wait until we reach England."

"Why not? Are you taking a walking tour as soon as we land?" She hurried to catch up with him, yet her voice was still scolding.

The ship rose on the crest of a wave and Simon

staggered, reaching out in disgust to lean on the side wall of the ship. This damn weakness of his! "I can't let Madeline see me like this."

"Madeline?"

He turned to the slight woman next to him, but saw instead Madeline. Her tall, slender figure. Her gleaming dark hair. A smile so warm and tender he was lost in it. Yet the vision lasted only a moment. It was elusive, as if the brisk winds and salty spray from the waves were too harsh for her delicate nature.

"She's the most beautiful woman ever created," Simon said simply. "We're going to be married when I get home."

The tossing of the ship brought him back to the present, back to his aching leg that could barely support him. He looked down at his stiff leg with anger and disgust. "How would you feel if the man you were going to marry came to you like this? Nothing but a cripple?"

"I should be glad that he was still alive."

Her voice was equally sharp and angry, and it awoke in Simon a sudden horror of what he'd said. The anger and impatience with his slow healing disappeared as he reached out to grasp her hand tightly. "I'm terribly sorry," he said. "I didn't mean to remind you of your loss like that."

"It doesn't matter." She brushed aside his apology, but her eyes still burned. "But you mustn't assume that Madeline would feel any differently. You may be doing her a grave injustice. If she loves you, a stiff leg surely will not matter."

Simon shook his head. "Not to you, perhaps.

24

You are strong and I admire your courage. But Madeline is different. She has been so sheltered, she could not be expected to cope with something like this."

"I see," Mrs. Smith said quietly. Her voice was cold and stilted and spoke her disapproval even though her words were vague. They reached a companionway and she stopped. "I think I had better get back to Teddy. Thank you for your company." Without waiting for his reply, she slipped through the opening and down the steps.

Simon frowned, the polite murmurings dying on his tongue as he watched until she was out of sight. He knew she had not understood about Madeline. Mrs. Smith was very different from the women he'd known in England. She was almost like a child in some ways, so open and trusting, not hiding her feelings behind the ritual of polite society. Yet she was also strong beyond her years from the trial she'd endured. But strength was not wisdom, and no matter how strong she might have been to endure those hardships, she could not begin to understand someone such as Madeline. Glad as Madeline might be to see him alive, she was too beautiful, too perfect, to be tied down to a cripple.

He began to walk again.

Chapter Two

A blinding curtain of rain was falling when the *Flying Arrow* reached Southampton, making the wait to disembark even more miserable. Catherine stood in the shelter of a companionway, clutching Teddy as she watched the slow-moving rituals of docking the ship. The town beyond them seemed gray and forbidding, uncaring of her arrival. Not a very auspicious beginning of the end of her journey, she thought, then scolded herself for being silly. The rain, the weary look of the town, had no effect on her journey. Her emotions were just as unsteady as the sea, and she mustn't let the worries drown her. How could things go wrong, after all? Hadn't she already proved her luck in meeting Simon?

He'd truly been a godsend during the trip, always there with a kind word and a sympathetic smile. She had clung to his support rather shamelessly, she feared, seeking out his company whenever Teddy's fussing or her own exhaustion threatened to overcome her. His gentle courtesies had helped her forget how alone she was and the desperateness of her journey.

When at last it was their turn to debark, Catherine held Teddy under her heavy woolen cloak while Simon took her arm to steady her. It was not until she had her feet firmly on the wooden dock that she recognized the sour worry in her stomach for what it was: fear. She'd grown used to leaning on Simon and was afraid of facing the rest of her journey alone. How weak she'd become! she told herself and, pushing back her thoughts, ordered her heart to be brave.

With an attempt at a smile she looked around her. "Why, this looks just like Halifax or Boston," she cried in mock disappointment.

Simon laughed and guided her through the crowd to find a coach. "What did you expect? I imagine most ports look similar."

"Somehow I had expected England to look a little different from home," she admitted with a smile. Her heart was obeying; it felt stronger with each passing moment.

Simon flagged down a coach. "The Red Lion Inn," he directed the driver as he opened the door for Catherine.

She took a deep breath; the moment was here. His company, his support, had been wonderful, but she was strong enough to be on her own. She did not need his smile for courage any longer. "I want to thank you for all you've done," she said quite properly. "But you mustn't worry any longer about me. I shall be fine." It was a replay of the same argument they'd been having for days and its outcome was no different this time either.

"We're both going to London. Why shouldn't we travel together?" he had always said, and did again as he helped her into the carriage.

Why shouldn't they? There were a million reasons, yet not a one she could tell him. How could she explain her fear of becoming too fond of his kindnesses? How could she admit to a growing dependency on his strength?

Or was it really his smile that drew her? That was a thread she had no desire to follow, and huddled in the corner of the coach, fussing over the sleeping Teddy. She'd buried her husband not that long ago. How could she be feeling warmth in the shadow of another man? And one that was betrothed to a woman he'd loved for years? Not that his Madeline sounded worthy to even be in the same room as him. Stop it! she cried to her heart. Madeline was another thread she would not follow. The coach pulled up to the inn and Catherine climbed out in relief, as if she were leaving her disturbing thoughts behind, clinging to the leather seats.

While they waited for their luggage to be brought from the ship, they had a hot meal. Simon had wanted to hire a private room for her to wait in, but Catherine preferred the common room with its bustling crowd of travelers. They watched the others, laughing and smiling over the antics of the motley collection of guests. Then another coach was ready and they were on their way to London.

One bumpy mile after another passed, and

28

Catherine grew weary of trying to fight her worries with conversation. Simon retreated into silence also, staring out the window as London drew ever closer. The crease in his forehead looked almost like worry to her, but how could that be? He would soon have his heart's desire, everything he'd ever wanted from life. She turned to stare out her own window.

That night she slept fitfully at the White Hart Inn, then gave herself up to the mindless monotony of the ride, her tension growing with each change of horses as she was pulled closer to London. It wasn't just leaving Simon's support that would be difficult, but this whole trip seemed suddenly fraught with danger. That rational decision she'd made a month before now seemed wildly impulsive. How could she have been so foolish as to leave her home for a foreign country and life amid strangers?

The small confines of the coach suddenly seemed to be suffocating. The drab leather walls were closing in on her, mocking her assumption that Edward's family would welcome her, or even be in a position to take her in. What if they were traveling on the Continent and not even home? Her own small store of money wasn't enough to support her and Teddy for any length of time, and not enough to get them to her mother's distant relatives in Boston if the trip to England proved to be a disaster.

None of these worries were new, yet never before had they seemed so threatening. She searched for a way to divert her attention. "Will Madeline be in London?" she asked Simon suddenly.

He started and turned from the window. "I don't

29

know. The season has certainly begun, so she may be in town with her father. In any case, I had planned to go to my grandmother's. She will know where Madeline is."

Catherine nodded, but his gaze drifted toward the window again, leaving her alone with her fears. "What of your parents?" she asked, fighting to draw his eyes back to her. "Do they live in London?"

"No, my mother died giving birth to my sister when I was four, and my father died a few months later. Since then, my sister and I have lived with my paternal grandmother, along with our cousin Nigel Marley," he said. The coach rounded a bend, and Simon grabbed hold of a strap to steady himself before continuing. "Once we reach London, I shall give you my grandmother's direction so you can reach me should you need to."

"I am certain that won't be necessary," she protested. Her worries were real, but her heart was allowed no weakening. "I have imposed on your generosity too much as it is."

But he had already turned to stare out the window, and she knew that he was lost in his thoughts of Madeline. She sighed, and looked down at Teddy, asleep in her arms. Surely any family whose eldest son had been killed would welcome that son's wife and child. But there were no thoughts that could bring her peace.

She and Simon reached London in the late afternoon. The trip that seemed so endless had suddenly sped by as they pulled into the courtyard of the

Royal George Inn. It looked much the same as any large inn, but it seemed to lack warmth. Was it her fears making it seem so or the bustle of departing and arriving coaches?

She gathered her things together, avoiding an answer to her question. There would be no putting off taking her leave of Simon now. He was eager to be off to seek out his Madeline, but she was grateful once they left the coach that he stayed long enough to secure her a room for the night.

He also paid for it, which she hadn't wanted at all, but somehow her argument against it was lost in the knowledge that in a few moments he'd be gone from her life. Don't be silly! her heart warned. Simon had been a good friend, but they both had their own roads to tread. Yet even as she summoned up the traces of a smile to send him on his way, she was aware of how precious their friendship had been. When was the last time she'd truly had such a friend? It had been a long time. Certainly Edward hadn't qualified as one though he should have been. With a shake of her head to chase the shadows from her voice, she bid Simon farewell calmly, her fears nowhere near her voice.

"Now, promise to come to me if things don't work out with your husband's family," Simon told her as they stood in the lower hallway of the inn. "I will find some way to help you."

She nodded and smiled, though she knew she wouldn't.

"Not that I expect I will need to," he went on. "They will take one look at the two of you and welcome you completely."

Somehow she kept her smile in place as her heart plummeted into her stomach as he picked up his hand luggage, then put one arm around her shoulder and hugged her. His light, brotherly kiss on her forehead did nothing to ease the wobbly state of her heart. "Good luck to you both, little Kate," he said cheerfully, and let her go.

A moment later he was gone and Catherine was alone. She hugged Teddy tightly to her breast. She was strong enough to manage, she told herself, and strong enough not to be jealous of Simon's devotion to Madeline. Catherine climbed the stairs to her room.

Simon did not notice many evidences of change in the city as he walked down Bond Street. The styles of clothes were different and he would have to see about replacing his wardrobe, but so much else looked the same. The buildings were still a mixture of shabbiness and pretention, as were the people, but still everything seemed to be smiling at him. Lord, it was good to be home!

He hailed a passing hackney and rode to Audley Street, noting with relief that the knocker was on his grandmother's door. After tossing an extra coin up to the driver—and earning an extra tip of the man's hat—Simon walked briskly up the stairs and rapped on the door with his cane. His leg was as strong as his happiness.

An elderly butler answered his knock, his wrinkled old face coming alive when he saw Simon standing there. "Mr. Bradford!" he cried, stepping aside for Simon to enter. "Won't the madam be surprised!"

"She is in, then, Benson?"

The butler nodded. "In the parlor. They're just having tea. Shall I announce you?"

Simon shook his head with a grin and handed Benson his hat, and his cane. "No, I think I will surprise them."

He walked across the foyer and up the long flight of stairs, his feet slowing with each step. It wasn't his injury coming back to mock his joy though. No, it was the memories that were assaulting him, the comfortable familiarity of the house. The handrail that he used to slide down was worn smooth by the years. The line of portraits marched up the steps with him, his great-uncle Benjamin's listing slightly to port as it always had. The smell of beeswax and oil was in the air, mingling with the spring aromas of tulips and daffodils from the vases in the hall above. He was home.

His heart was ready to burst with excitement as he crossed the upper hallway with slow, careful steps. Stopping for a moment outside the parlor, he heard his grandmother's voice through the closed door. How he had missed her, missed her understanding and generous laughter. But then the mingle of another, softer voice was heard and he hoped that there weren't a number of guests there. It would be hard to make pleasant small talk while wanting to catch up on all the family news. And wanting to ask about Madeline. Taking a deep breath, Simon pushed open the door and stepped into the room.

His grandmother was sitting in the velvet-covered chair across from the door and saw him instantly. She stopped in mid-speech, her mouth open and her eyes glittering with sudden wateriness. She rose unsteadily to her feet. "Simon!"

He was across the floor in a few long strides and took her into his arms. "Hello, Grandmother," he said, kissing her cheek. The skin felt dry and shriveled to his lips, her body seemed unbelievably frail against his. When had she grown so old?

"Where have you come from?" she demanded. Her voice was weaker than he remembered also, and her eyes were weary, as if she'd been ill. "Why didn't you write so we could expect you?"

He let go of her, slipping his hands down to grasp hers. "I'm not much of a writer," he said. There had been little he could write about that would not have caused her worry. He let her sink back into her chair. Her movements seemed weak.

"But the last we heard was from some corporal who had returned from Montreal. He said you had been dreadfully wounded." Her searching eyes never left his as they probed and pushed, trying to read answers to her unspoken questions.

Simon cursed under his breath. He should have realized that they might have heard. Was that what had caused her to age so? "Well, you can see that I am still in one piece," he said, shrugging off his injuries as if they had been greatly exaggerated. He felt the presence of another person and was grateful that his grandmother would not be able to press her questions, even if it meant postponing his own mission. He turned with a polite smile and found himself staring into Madeline's face.

"Madeline." It was a gasp of pure ecstasy as the world stood still.

She smiled at him, more beautiful than he remembered. Her dark brown hair gleamed with hidden fire and framed her face exquisitely, her smooth skin seemed paler than possible with just the faintest blush of rose on her cheeks. Her blue eyes were deep and entrancing, holding him prisoner with their mystery.

"Oh, Simon, we were so worried about you," she purred softly, and glided across the floor toward him.

Her black dress made her seem taller and more slender, a fragile, spiritlike presence he feared would disappear into his dreams as she so often had in the past.

"We tried so hard to find out what had happened, but no one seemed to know." She stopped right before him, her blue eyes staring up into his, weaving a tapestry he couldn't understand. "Welcome home, Simon," she whispered. Reaching up, she kissed him lightly on the cheek, the gentlest breath of springtime on the thawing winter ground. But like the kiss of springtime, the touch warmed him, stirring the love and the need that had kept him alive through those dark hours.

He took her hand gently, cupping it in his own

like a rare and delicate bird. "I thought of you so often while I was gone."

He raised her hand to his lips. Behind him, the parlor door opened and he heard with vague awareness someone enter the room. No one mattered though, now that he had found his Madeline.

"I assume that is a brotherly kiss that you're giving my wife."

Simon's breath caught as the words shot across the room, freezing his blood with winds more bitter than those that stole through the cracks in that old hospital-church in Montreal. His joy died a sudden death; the warmth was gone from his heart as numbness took its place. He turned slowly, painfully, to find his cousin Nigel in the doorway. Dressed in pale blue and mauve, Nigel was leaning against the doorpost in a pose of total boredom. Mocking laughter gleamed in his eyes as if he could sense the pain and shock his words had caused.

"Your wife?" Simon repeated, and turned back to Madeline. His eyes begged with her to disagree, to laugh it off as a joke.

But she just smiled gently and moved away from him. His hand was left empty and cold, just like his heart. A bitterness seeped through his blood, leaving desolation in its wake. Madeline had married Nigel? But why?

Nigel straightened up and sauntered across the room. He took Madeline's hand, kissing it in the same spot that Simon had, and Simon felt the chill deepen.

"You and Nigel are married?" he asked.

Madeline's smile seemed apologetic, almost pleading for his understanding, his blessing, but Nigel's harsh laugh washed away any easing of pain Madeline's eyes might have offered. "My dear boy, things have changed while you were out playing soldier. Someone had to take charge of the family's affairs, and I fear that duty fell to me."

Nigel took Madeline's arm and led her over to the settee. Simon's eyes followed their steps, watching the way Nigel patted her hand, the way he kept her close to him, his every movement designed to remind Simon that she belonged to him now. The numbness in Simon's heart began to change to a slow-burning anger. What trickery was this? He should challenge Nigel to a duel; he should kidnap Madeline and run away with her as they had tried years back.

"And just when did—" Simon took a step forward, seeing only the fading of his dreams. Seeing only his future, empty and meaningless without Madeline. His leg was more firmly grounded in reality though and bumped sharply into the side of a chair. The blinding streak of pain made him cry out, but also brought him back to reason.

"Simon?" His grandmother jumped to her feet, fear clutching her voice and eyes.

"I'm fine. It was nothing." He forced a quiet, a calm into his voice that he didn't feel, and limped to a nearby chair.

The throbbing agony in his leg matched the pain in his heart, but his blinding anger faded somewhat. Madeline's eyes seemed to reflect the mockery in Nigel's, and Simon turned away, angry with himself for his sudden disloyal thought. Something must have happened; somehow she must have been forced to marry Nigel. She would not have abandoned their love otherwise. He would wait to find out the truth before he let his anger consume him. But in the meantime he would not let anyone see his hurt. He took a deep breath and turned to his grandmother.

"Where is Anne? I expected she would be in town with you."

The old woman shook her head. "Hadn't you heard? Edward died."

The news was startling and Simon turned toward Madeline. "I am terribly sorry," he said softly. His eyes held hers for a moment; it was almost as if they were alone. "It must have been an awful blow to your father. I know how proud he was of Edward."

Madeline just nodded, her eyes filling with sudden tears that mirrored her grief. Simon's jaw tightened. If only he had the right to comfort her!

"Actually, I was surprised at how hard Anne took the news," his grandmother told him, drawing his eyes and thoughts from Madeline. "I knew she was fond of him, but I never expected her to go to pieces as she did. She wouldn't leave Bradleigh for months after his death, and I had the hardest time persuading her to go to Bath with the Johnstones for a few weeks. Perhaps now that you are home, you can cheer her up."

"I shall try, but I'm not sure a brother's concern

will help," Simon assured her.

"Nonsense. She thinks the world of you, and your presence will shake us all from the doldrums."

Was it that easy to recover from the loss of a loved one? he wondered, but just nodded again, his eyes avoiding Madeline as he reached for the tea his grandmother had poured for him.

"I think you're presuming too much, Grandmother," Nigel said with a quiet laugh. His voice was as mocking as his manner. "Cousin Anne may not want to forget her love for Edward. The Bradfords all seem to have this strange penchant for undying love."

"Oh, Nigel, don't be absurd," his grandmother said, her voice suddenly weary with old battles.

Simon's eyes met those of his cousin. "What is that supposed to mean?" Simon's voice was quiet, his anger masked.

But Nigel's smile was all innocence. "Didn't you come back expecting to find Madeline waiting for you? I seem to remember a certain passionately written missive in which you vowed your eternal love."

"Nigel!" Madeline's protest was almost sincere, except for the hint of a smile playing about her lips. "You weren't supposed to have seen that."

The frozen numbness that had taken hold of Simon's heart at finding Madeline married was gone now, burned away with the sudden intensity of anger. His eyes narrowed as he took in the picture of Nigel and Madeline, the same mockery in both their eyes.

39

But Mrs. Bradford only laughed off the taunts as if they hadn't been spoken. "Whatever are you talking about? Simon did not expect Madeline to be waiting for him. They were not betrothed. You make him sound like some moonstruck youth."

Nigel's eyes mocked as he bowed politely toward Simon. "I do beg your pardon, Cousin."

Simon said nothing for a moment. The need to deny his pain, to pretend that he wasn't bleeding inside, was so strong it robbed him of his voice. He took a deep breath and pushed slow, careful words from his mouth. He wanted nothing more than to strike back against those who had hurt him. "You seem to have gotten the wrong idea somewhere. I am quite glad that Madeline did not hold me to that ridiculous pledge of love that I made as a youth. It would have made things extremely awkward."

His grandmother reached her hand over toward him. "Oh, Simon, you mean you have found someone else? How wonderful!"

Simon started in surprise. He'd meant he no longer cared about Madeline, not that he had fallen in love elsewhere. "Grandmother—"

"Tell us all about her," his grandmother demanded with eagerness. She suddenly looked years stronger, her face aglow with happiness for him and the weariness gone from her eyes. "Did you meet her in Canada? You can't know how happy this makes me that you've found someone of your own."

"Actually, I—"

"Now, if we can just get Anne settled, I can die

in peace," she said with a satisfied sigh.

"Grandmother! What kind of talk is this?" Simon cried, but knew even as he protested that it was something that had been on her mind. He could see in her eyes that she was feeling her age. What would it matter if they all thought some mysterious woman had caught his eye? His decision was made before he'd even thought about it. If it made his grandmother happy, he would find a way to string the story along until he could gently ease her down. He wouldn't mind taking Nigel and Madeline's mockery down a peg or two either.

"I'm so happy for you, Simon. We'll want to hear all about her," his grandmother gushed with a quick squeeze of his hand, then a frown raced across her brow. "Oh, fiddlesticks, that sounds like Lady Atwell arriving for tea. There's no time to talk now."

The door opened and the town's worst gossip-monger swept in. The interruption was welcome, but this old battle-ax was the last person in the world he wished to see. She'd never forgiven Simons' grandmother for catching Geoffrey Bradford's eye years before and took delight in trying to best Mrs. Bradford.

"So you came back at last, eh, Simon?" Lady Atwell cackled with a quick glance at Madeline as she took her seat. "Just about everybody's forgotten your scandalous elopement, but maybe you can refresh their memories. Especially with the two of you living in the same house."

"Adelia, how can you say such things?" Mrs.

41

Bradford smiled away the waspish words. "That was years ago, when both Simon and Madeline were children."

The old woman twisted in her chair to keep a beady eye on Nigel and Madeline. "Speaking of children, when are you and your wife going to start a nursery? Better keep a close eye on your garden so no weeds stray in."

A flicker in Nigel's eyes told Simon his cousin's anger was woken up, but Mrs. Bradford just shook her head at the old woman. "If you're looking for some scandal to spread, I'm afraid you're in the wrong house," she told Lady Atwell smoothly. "Simon and Madeline are cousins now, nothing more. In fact, Simon himself has married."

Simon had been ready to reach for his cup of tea, but his hand froze in midair. What? How in the world had his grandmother reached that conclusion? His eyes darted to his grandmother, trying to stop this misunderstanding before it grew any larger, but Mrs. Bradford was smiling benignly at her guest.

"Oh, and when did this happen?" Lady Atwell wanted to know. Her voice reeked with suspicion and the desire for scandal. "I don't remember any notice in the *Times*."

"Uh, grandmother—" Simon said with quiet urgency, only to be ignored.

"I am certain that will be rectified soon," his grandmother said smoothly. "She's a lovely girl."

"You've met her?" Lady Atwell asked.

"I feel as if I have," his grandmother insisted.

"Simon's letters have been full of her."

Simon choked at the blatant lie, and glanced at Nigel and Madeline. Neither of them looked about to expose his grandmother's fabrication, but then, neither did they know how false it was. What the devil was he going to do? If Lady Atwell found out his grandmother had made the whole story up, she'd never let her live it down. Of course, his grandmother wasn't really to blame. He'd chosen to let them think that he'd met someone else, claiming it was for his grandmother's sake. But it had really been his own stupid pride that had gotten them into this mess, and it was up to him to find a way out. And right now that was the door. He rose to his feet.

"If you all will excuse me, I think I'd better be on my way. It's been a long day."

"Simon," his grandmother protested. "Where are you going? Aren't you going to move back in here? We've hardly had a chance to talk."

"I still have some luggage to track down and some errands to run," he said smoothly. "I'll see you tomorrow, I promise." He kissed her on the cheek, then bowed to Lady Atwell, Madeline, and Nigel.

"That boy never did know how to stay out of trouble," Lady Atwell said loudly as he went to the door. "I'll wager we'll have something to talk about before the week is out."

Simon realized he was sweating as the door closed behind him.

Lord Edward Killian was not a man to be taken lightly. His moods were of constant concern among the servants of his household, for misreading them might cost one his job. Kendall, his lordship's butler, had remained in his employ for many years by his sole virtue of sensing trouble whenever it approached and then becoming invisible.

When the young lady appeared at the door asking to speak to his lordship, Kendall was uneasy. He considered sending a footman into the drawing room, where his lordship was having tea, but then remembered that Master Michael was in with him and that always put Lord Killian in a good mood. It would be safe to go in himself.

However, Michael Corbett-Smith had failed the old butler this time. He was standing up, facing his father, who was in a towering rage.

"But Edward always came with me," Lord Killian cried. "Now that you are my heir, you must."

"Being your heir has nothing to do with it," Michael snapped. "I do not choose to be a member of Prinny's inner circle. I have no interests in common with any of them and would much rather be back at the estate."

Lord Killian shuddered slightly as he took in the figure of his son. Michael had never put much importance on fashion, although he was tall and slender and could wear the tight-fitting coats and breeches that were in style. Instead, he chose loose-fitting buckskin jackets and dark-colored pants. When he did concede to fashion's dictates, he always chose the simplest styles and the dullest colors. He did not even have a trained man trim and style his wavy black hair, but had his valet cut it when it got too long.

"You don't seem to realize the importance of your position now that Edward is no longer with us," Lord Killian said with pronounced patience. "You have a duty, a responsibility to this family, and all it has stood for over the ages."

Michael looked bored. "That is all nonsense. I was a Corbett-Smith before he died and I'm still one today. I can't see why I must dress like a jackass and prance about in town just because I'm the only son left."

"You are a leader of society now!" his father insisted, pounding on the desk before him for emphasis. "People look up to you for guidance."

"You mean that if I wear blue satin breeches and a purple waistcoat, people will respect me more? No, thank you. Society and you will have to take me or leave me as I am." He turned and strode toward the door.

"Michael, I forbid you to leave London!"

"Is that how you treat a leader of society?" Michael's mocking laughter angered his father even more. He pulled open the door, and found the butler about to knock. "Ah, do come in, Kendall. We were just finished." He slipped past the man, disappearing from his father's sight.

Kendall was rapidly regretting his decision to see his lordship himself, for it was obvious he was livid with anger. "There's a young lady who wishes to see

45

you, my lord," he said with an apologetic cough.

Lord Killian glared at him. "I don't want to see any young lady. Send her on her way."

Kendall coughed quietly again. "Yes, my lord, I did try, but she said it was most important and had to do with Master Edward."

Sighing impatiently, Lord Killian waved his hand. "I shall give her two minutes, no more. And it had best be important, Kendall," he added darkly.

"Yes, my lord." Kendall bowed and raised his eyes in supplication as he went back into the hallway. A few moments later he was back with a young woman. He showed her into the room, then left quickly, closing the door behind him.

Lord Killian stared at the creature before him, unable to believe that his butler had actually allowed her in. She was very small and thin as an undernourished child and dressed in a rag of a black dress. She looked like a scullery maid, except that she was obviously far too puny to be of much use.

"What do you want?" he snapped, his eyebrows coming together fiercely.

A quick look of apprehension crossed her face, then she took a step forward. Her hands were clenched in front of her. "Lord Killian?"

He nodded curtly.

She took a deep breath, then looked him straight in the eye. "My name is Catherine Smith. I was married to your son, Edward," she said.

Lord Killian stared at her, the rage at her audacity growing until it was a pounding roar in his ears.

46

"You were what?" he thundered.

"I was Edward's wife," she repeated. "I assume that he must have written and told you about our marriage. I wrote you myself after his death."

Whom was she trying to fool? Edward would never marry a nothing like her, an unfashionable stick of a woman. Edward knew his place in society and knew style. The atrociousness of her clothes alone would be enough to convince him she was lying, even if there weren't hundreds of other reasons not to believe her.

"I received letters from my son regularly, and there never was any mention of a wife."

She had the acting skill to look slightly surprised. "Perhaps he meant it as a surprise."

Lord Killian had met far more experienced tricksters than this little doxy and not been fooled by them. This woman must think him the veriest greenhorn to be taken in by such a preposterous story. While his anger was still strong at her insult to Edward's memory, he relaxed slightly, enjoying the chance to expose her as the charlatan she was.

"Knowing my son, a surprise does not seem likely. We were extremely close and I know he would not marry without telling me."

"Yet, he did."

"So you say. If you even knew him, you were merely a little diversion to pass the time. How convenient that you should appear when he is no longer here to tell us the truth!"

The woman's eyes flashed with almost believable anger. "I have told you the truth. We were married a year ago last March. In a church in Halifax! Why would I lie about such a thing?"

"Why indeed?" he snarled, advancing a step. The game had gone on long enough. "You must think me a fool to be taken in by such a Banbury tale. All I have to do is look at you to know my son never married you. He was a Killian, and we, young lady, are very aware of our position in society. He would never marry some plain little nobody from Canada. He had a duty to marry well, and he was not about to forget it. As a matter of fact, he was betrothed to such a young lady here in England, so you see, your little scheme has failed!"

She paled but didn't flinch. "I have no little scheme, as you put it. Edward and I were married and I have our marriage lines to prove it." Digging into her reticule, she pulled out a folded piece of paper and held it out to him, but he made no move to take another piece of her trickery. She took another step closer, and reluctantly he took it from her.

He opened the paper and glanced briefly at it before crumpling it in his fist. "A clever forgery, I'll admit, but not clever enough for me." He let it fall to the ground. "You'd need far more than some dirty piece of paper to convince me that you are really Edward's wife."

She retrieved the paper, and smoothed the wrinkles out, then folded it up again. Her hands were trembling, and he had to give her credit for an excellent performance.

"And just what would it take to convince you?"

she asked, her voice quivering with just the right amount of emotion. "Would you like to see his son?"

"Ah, so there's a brat involved, is there? I should have guessed." It was foolish of him not to have seen it from the beginning. "Are you hoping that the little bastard would soften me into providing funds for your living? Or are you just bitter because you were left with the brat and no wedding ring?"

Seeing that her little plan had no chance for success, the woman stuffed the marriage lines back into her reticule as she obviously prepared for her dramatic exit.

"He is not a bastard. He is your grandson, but you don't deserve to see him." Tears were running down her cheeks. "You have insulted us in every way imaginable and I will never forget it. Someday you will be sorry that you have acted this way."

She turned and practically ran from the room. Lord Killian laughed. The fact that she thought she could convince him that she was married to Edward gave him the first real amusement he'd had since his son's death.

Chapter Three

Catherine angrily brushed the tears from her cheeks as she fled from Grosvenor Square. She was aware of the curious glances from the people she passed, but she resolutely kept her head high. In spite of the terrifying question of the future, there was something else that disturbed her more. Why hadn't Edward told his family that he had married?

If she had known that he was corresponding with his family, she would have found the absence of a letter to her quite strange. But he had always fobbed off her questions with excuses of poor mail service during the war and the ease with which a letter could go astray. Like the naive fool she had been, she had been satisfied.

There also was the question of his fiancée in England. Once they were married, why hadn't he broken off the engagement? Why would he keep writing to his family as if nothing had changed?

Catherine stopped suddenly, a sudden wrenching pain in her heart. Perhaps, to him, nothing of importance had changed. Maybe he had had no intention of bringing her back to England with him.

She began to walk again, but more slowly, instinctively retracing her steps back to the inn. People were bustling about her, some selling wares, others hurrying to some destination, but she took little notice of them as she went back to the time when she had met Edward.

The war between England and the States had broken out, and she and her father had left Boston to settle comfortably in Halifax. Although most of her father's assets had been left behind, he had a great number of business acquaintances in Canada and they had been quite generous with their loans while he worked to get his money from the States.

With borrowed funds he had rented a huge house in the best district and filled both their wardrobes with the latest fashions. He had become the intimate of the governor and the commander of the British regiment stationed there, and anyone else of importance. Entertaining lavishly, invitations to his parties had been greatly sought after.

It had been at one of those parties that she had met Edward. Somehow her father knew which of the soldiers came from influential families in England and had been careful to include them.

Edward made a striking picture in his uniform. He was tall and his dark features were most attractive to the ladies. Unaccountably to her, he sought out her company and soon became a regular guest at their house. Her father was terribly fond of him and even loaned him money time after time when he found himself badly dipped. When Edward pro-

51

posed, Catherine was ecstatic, if slightly unbelieving. She could not imagine why he would want to marry her, not when he had all the young women of Halifax to choose from.

Things went quite smoothly for the first months after the marriage. They lived with her father in the huge house, Edward staying at the post only when necessary. When she became pregnant, she sensed Edward's withdrawal but paid little attention, for her father was ill. When he died, her romantic bubble burst.

Creditors came from every corner, demanding that the huge loans be repaid. Catherine, having no head for business, referred them all to Edward, who soon learned that her father never had any hope of regaining the lost funds. He had borrowed unscrupulously, knowing that he would never repay any of it.

After selling what she could to repay a few of the loans, she and Edward moved to a tiny house near the army post. She did not mind the move as much as he had, and relations between them worsened. She heard rumors that he was seeing other women, but didn't have the courage to confront him with the information. Or, perhaps, the last few months numbed her into insensibility. Then, suddenly, Edward was dead also.

Catherine had few friends after her father's unscrupulous behavior, and Edward forbade her to mingle with people from the post, so she was quite alone. Staying for the while in the tiny house, she tried to decide if she should go back to Boston to her mother's family. After Teddy was born though, she knew she had to take him back to England, to Edward's family. That was what Edward would have wanted.

Now that she was in England though, she knew she had been wrong. Edward had never really cared for her. Maybe he had been fooled by her father's apparent wealth and lost interest in her only when he had learned that there was no fortune for her to inherit. Or more likely, her father had blackmailed Edward into the marriage over his gambling debts. If Edward had not died when he had, how would he have managed to return to England without her?

Before an answer arrived, Catherine was back at the Royal George with more immediate problems demanding solutions. She had to get Teddy from the innkeeper's wife and face the question of their future. Her steps lagged slightly as she walked across the inn yard, and pulled open the door.

Her gaze faltered in the dim interior, and she walked slowly until she could see again. By that time she was standing next to the common room and, glancing in, found a man with his back to her resembling Simon.

That was ridiculous, she told herself. She was so alone that she was seeing similarities that weren't there. She wanted to feel that Simon was close by even though she knew he would be happily surrounded by his family by this time. Yet even as she thought that, her feet led her into the room.

A man at a nearby table glared at her, but she barely noticed. She suspected that in England, well-bred young ladies did not frequent the common rooms of inns. Customs had not been so rigid back home though, so she did not hesitate to walk over to the man she had seen. It was indeed Simon.

"Simon!" She was so surprised to find him that she sat down on the bench across from him. "What are you doing?"

He frowned at her. "Drinking," he said simply, and poured himself another glass from the half-empty bottle of brandy before him. He was about to raise the glass to his lips, but stopped. "Would you like one, too?"

"Of course not. And you look like you have had quite enough already." He was still dressed in his uniform, but it no longer looked crisp and fresh.

"No, I'm afraid I haven't." His smile was unpleasant. "You see, I am still quite sober and that was not my goal."

Catherine leaned closer to him. She could see the pain in his eyes and wondered what had gone wrong. He had been so happy earlier. "What happened, Simon? Did you see your grandmother?"

He took a long drink of the brandy and put the glass down in front of him, turning it slightly in a wet spot on the table. "Oh, yes. I saw her. She was quite glad to see me." He took another drink and Catherine was ready to shake him in frustration.

"Obviously, you aren't drinking yourself into oblivion because your grandmother was glad to see you. What about Madeline? Did your grandmother know where Madeline was?"

"Would have been hard not to know, she was sitting right across the room from her."

Catherine leaned back. That had to be it. "So you saw her?"

Simon appeared not to have heard her, for he was staring down at the glass in his hand, holding it so tightly that Catherine feared it would burst. Then suddenly he looked up at her, his eyes raw with grief. "Oh, yes, I saw her."

"And are you still going to marry her?" she prompted.

He laughed bitterly. "I fear her husband might object to that."

"Her husband? Oh, Simon, I am so sorry." She wanted to reach out and comfort him, but this wasn't the same man she had gotten to know on board the ship. There was a wall of bitterness around him that she didn't know how to break down.

"I was a fool to think she would have waited for me. But did it have to be Nigel?"

"Your cousin? So they'll be living in the same house as you?" How awful for him!

Simon poured himself another drink. "Won't that be cozy?" His voice was harsh with forced amusement that fooled neither of them.

Though Catherine ached for him, she was more concerned with his actions. He seemed intent on drinking himself into a stupor, and that would help nothing. He hadn't seen Madeline for a few years, could his feelings for her have been so strong that he couldn't even bear to be with his family? "I know it must be an awful blow, Simon, but this is your first night home. Shouldn't you be with your grandmother instead of here drinking?" She put her hand over his. "Go home, Simon."

"I can't," he said, and took another drink.

"Of course you can," she told him, keeping her voice as brisk and bracing as possible. "If Madeline married another, then she didn't care enough about you. You are better off without her."

His glare was angry. Had she gone too far? "I am not here sulking," he snapped. "I'm here because I made an ass of myself and I cannot go back."

She stared at him until he put down the glass with a loud sigh. "That fool Nigel kept smirking and laughing at me until I couldn't take it anymore."

"So you shot him," Catherine said with a hint of a smile. "And now Madeline's a widow?"

Simon frowned. "It might have been better had I done that. No, instead I told them I was glad Madeline hadn't waited for me."

"That's not so bad."

"Grandmother assumed that I meant I was married also and announced it to a tongue-wagging old fool who came for tea."

Catherine laughed suddenly, but stopped at his frown. "It really is rather funny," she tried to make him see.

"It is impossible. How can I go back there now? Grandmother's expecting me to produce a wife."

So he was drinking himself into oblivion because he was embarrassed. How silly and how sad. A stupid reason to waste even a moment of time with a loved one. "It might be awkward, but certainly if you explained things to her in private . . ."

"You've been crying," he accused her in an angry voice.

Catherine stared at him, startled by his abrupt

56

change of subject. Her hands gently touched her cheeks, where she felt the heat of his gaze. Her skin was still damp and her eyes felt red and raw.

"And where is Teddy?" he demanded, looking around as if he expected to see him at the next table drinking ale.

"With the innkeeper's wife," Catherine said as she rose to her feet, all her own problems returning with sudden force. If only they were as simply solved as Simon's. "And it is time that I got him. I never expected to be this long."

She started to move from the table but Simon grabbed her hand. "Sit down," he ordered, but not unkindly.

Catherine hesitated for a moment, the pain of her visit still aching in her heart, but then did as he asked and sank back into her seat. She could not look at him though, and just stared down at her hands.

"I assume that your visit to your husband's family did not go as you had hoped," Simon said quietly.

She shook her head. There was no way she would repeat to him all those awful things Lord Killian had said to her. And it was not Simon's problem. He had taken on too many of her burdens on the trip over; it was time to free him of that responsibility.

"Were they in London? Or were you unable to find them?"

"Oh, I found them." She looked away at the shelves of pewter and copper mugs on the far wall and remembered a silver drinking cup her father had given to Edward when they had become engaged.

"Are you and Teddy going there to live?"

She shook her head again. That drinking cup had brought in enough to pay the midwife who had helped at Teddy's birth and the neighbor woman who had looked in on her often during her recovery.

She cleared her throat in an effort to clear her mind of the clutter of old memories. "No, actually we are making other plans right now." She would keep it vague. Let him think she was not alone and not his responsibility anymore.

Simon's eyes were hard as they stared at her and she avoided them, fearing he had the power to see her thoughts. He reached over and took her hand tightly in his, as if by doing so he could force the truth from her. "Are they going to help you in any way?"

The pressure of his hand and the steady onslaught of his gaze was too much for her. Why were his eyes always so kind? How could they awaken such warmth and hope in her? She was strong, she knew she was, yet when Simon was near, her spine turned to pudding.

"No," she finally admitted, barely loud enough for him to hear.

"That's marvelous!"

He sounded so genuinely pleased that Catherine stared at him in horror. He was grinning back at her.

"We can solve both of our problems at once, then!"

"We can?"

58

"All we have to do is get married," he explained. "Then I will have a wife and you and Teddy will have a home."

"But that's insane!" she cried, and pulled her hand away from his. His logic frightened her as did the prospect of security at the expense of his friendship. As did the sudden leap of joy in her heart that had nothing to do with security or friendship. "It's all that brandy talking. You don't know what you're saying."

"I know exactly what I'm saying," he snapped, and reached for her hand again. "What choice do you have? Can you support yourself and Teddy? Do you have funds to last you through the month here at the inn?"

His manner seemed suddenly cruel and her eyes filled with tears. "No."

With a sigh that seemed to soften the anger from him, he took her by the arm and led her out of the common room. They went up to her room in silence.

"I did not mean to upset you," he apologized quietly. The hall was deserted and he pushed the door to her room open. "I have no idea what your life was like in America, but your situation here is quite serious. Without any relations that you can turn to, you have very few choices. Marriage is the obvious one, since few employers would allow you to keep Teddy with you, assuming you even earned enough to support both of you."

Catherine said nothing, but just sank into the hard chair by the window and stared down at the busy inn yard. "I am quite aware of my precarious position," she said after a moment of silence to gain her strength and arrange her thoughts. "But I do not feel so desperate that I could accept your offer knowing how it would hurt you eventually."

"What the devil does that mean?"

She took a deep breath and turned to face him. The kindness in his face was harder to view with dispassion than the courtyard below. "I am not ignorant of the ways of English society. It is obvious from your manners and dress that you are a member of the gentry. Marriage to a nobody like myself would hurt the good name of your family." She hoped he would understand and cease this foolish discussion before her heart started to remind her of the sweetness of his smile.

But he just stared at her. "Where did you ever get such fool ideas?" Then his look of confusion disappeared. "Is that what they said to you?"

Catherine turned back to the window, to the safety away from his eyes. "It hardly matters how I know it. Marriage to me is out of the question, and when you are more sober, you will be relieved that I refused you."

"I don't know why you think that I am foxed." His laugh was more bitter than amused. "I assure you that it takes more than just a few brandies to cast me away, and there is nothing about you that would disgrace me."

"Oh, Simon," she sighed impatiently, and rose to her feet. Her heart clamored for her to say yes, to fall into his arms and seek the safety that surely lay there. But her mind was stronger, more determined to make him see reason.

"Your clothes are abominable, I'll admit," he went on. She followed his glance down her much-mended dress. "We will have to do something about them. My family would never believe that I would allow you to dress like that."

"These are my mourning clothes, you know," she reminded him quietly.

His lips twisted. "Mourning rags, more likely. My wife would never be seen in such shabby attire."

Catherine bit her lip and looked away. These were the same clothes that she had worn since her father died, yet Edward never objected to them. Her own husband had not cared that she looked like a beggar, while a comparative stranger did.

Simon must have seen her tears. "I'm sorry," he saw awkwardly. "I did not mean to criticize you or your husband. I am certain that he provided for you the best that he could."

She swallowed her tears and sat down again. Edward was not a subject that she could discuss just now. "This is impossible. You must see that."

"I would never have suspected you to be cowardly," he scolded. Pulling a chair close to hers, he sat down also. "It took a lot of courage to leave your home and come here. You can't become faint-hearted now."

She closed her eyes to the temptation of his smile and leaned her head back. It would be so nice to give in to his pleading, to forget all her troubles and let him worry about them. He was the type of man she'd always dreamed about marrying, sensitive and strong, someone who'd deserve her respect as well as her love, but she couldn't do it. He was upset and making wild offers he would regret soon. She had to remain strong and refuse, for his sake.

"It would not work," she sighed. "You don't know me."

"You would be taking an equal risk."

"But I wouldn't fit into your life here," she pleaded. "I grew up in a less restricted society. My mistakes will hurt you."

Simon laughed and took her hand. "You are grasping wildly at any excuse and you know it. Now, tell me, can you read?"

She stared at him in bewilderment, trying to ignore the flutterings in her stomach at the touch of his hand. "Yes, of course."

"Not 'of course.' Many people can't read. Can you play the pianoforte?"

"A little."

"Can you use silverware?"

She was becoming faintly annoyed. "Yes."

"Are you likely to play fast and loose with other men once we are married?"

"That's insulting," she cried, and jumped to her feet. "How could you suspect such a thing?"

He grinned. "You were the one that was certain you were going to disgrace me. I was just trying to determine how you were likely to do so."

She sat down slowly. "And?"

"I haven't found the way yet," he smiled. "Now, let us be serious. I shall get the special license tonight, so we can be married in the morning. Then we will go to my grandmother's. Have you any other clothes?"

"I have a few dresses that I had worn before Father died, but they would be hopelessly out of style in Canada now. They would be even worse here."

She walked over to her trunk, which was against one wall. After searching through it for a moment, she took out several dresses. One was a formal dress of heavy white satin trimmed with wide bands of French lace and tiny seed pearls. She had kept it because it was her wedding dress, but she did not tell that to Simon, and merely laid it across her bed in silence.

Next she unfolded a deep blue walking dress. It was deceptively simple in the Empire style with narrow ruffs around the neck, but the material had been expertly cut and it fit her beautifully. The soft folds of the fabric emphasized her slender figure while the deep blue color matched her eyes. The other dresses were simple muslins for day wear.

Simon walked over to look at them. "This one should do nicely," he said, indicating the blue one. "It may be a little out of style, but I doubt that Grandmother or Madeline will even notice."

She smiled without his confidence. They would notice; she was sure Madeline, at least, would notice everything. Not that it mattered though, she hadn't—and wouldn't—agree to this insanity. She'd tell Simon once and for all that she wouldn't marry him. But before she could say anything, someone knocked at the door. It was the innkeeper's wife and Teddy.

"I thought you was back," she said, holding the baby out for Catherine to take. "He was an angel."

"Thank you so much for your help." Catherine took Teddy from the woman and held him tightly, her love for him and her fear of the future washing over her together. He was all that was precious and of value in her life, and maybe for his sake she ought to take the desperate gamble. What other choices did she have that wouldn't hurt him far more than her?

"What's *he* doing in here?" the innkeeper's wife demanded with sudden anger. Catherine looked up to find the woman pointing at Simon. "This here's a respectable inn."

The woman's unexpected attack was enough to cause Catherine's careful upbringing to be forgotten. It was one too many accusations for the day. "How dare you speak to me that way!" Catherine cried. "This gentleman here is—"

"Her husband," Simon finished for her, suddenly at her side. "And I certainly will not tolerate such disrespect."

"Your husband?" The woman looked at the two of them uncertainly, then focused on Catherine. "I thought you said you was a widow?"

"What you think is of no importance," Simon snapped. "If my wife cannot be treated with respect here, we will go to some other inn."

"Oh, no, m'lord." She became apologetic. "It were just a mistake. I didn't mean no harm." Simon continued to glare at her as she turned to Catherine abjectly. "Is there anything I can do for you?"

Catherine glanced at Simon's forbidding face and the woman's anxious one and felt a little impish devil inside her. "I would like a bath."

"Right away, m'lady," the woman assured her.

"With plenty of hot water."

The woman's head bobbed up and down in agreement as she hurried down the stairs.

Catherine giggled and turned to Simon. "I can see that your presence does make a difference. Just a few hours ago that same woman was full of excuses when I asked for a bath."

"That is because you are far too easy to take advantage of," he snapped, sounding highly irritated for some reason.

He went to pick up his cane. "I shall try to get the license now," he said coldly. "Why don't you get a few hours rest? I will come back about eight o'clock and we can dine together."

The gentle, caring companion he'd been a few moments earlier was gone, replaced by someone dark and brooding, whose eyes gave no clue to the anger swirling within him. She sighed and watched as he walked back toward the door.

"Simon!" She reached across him to shut the door softly as he opened it. "If you have changed your mind, I will understand."

For a moment he stood facing the door, his back rigid and forbidding, then he turned slowly to face her. "I did not mean to be curt with you. I just realized that I, too, was guilty of taking advantage of your kind nature, and gave no thought to how painfully this must be reminding you of your other marriage." His voice was that of the gentle, kind man she had come to know and trust.

She put her hand on his arm. "I think if we are to make any kind of life together, you must understand that to me, my other marriage is over. Certainly some things will remind me of it, but those memories need not be painful, nor can they be avoided."

Simon nodded. "You must have loved him very much." He leaned forward to kiss her forehead lightly. His touch was warm and comforting. "Get some rest. I will be back in a few hours."

Chapter Four

"I don't know, Madeline," Mrs. Bradford sighed as they stood in the doorway of the bedroom that had been prepared for Simon and his wife. "I really think I ought to have moved from the large room and taken this one myself."

"Now, don't be silly." Madeline's smile was as sweet as it could be. "That has always been your room. Why should you give it up just because Simon is back?" There had never been any thought of giving it up for her and Nigel, Madeline thought, but her smile only deepened slightly.

"I just hope they like this room," the older woman sighed as she glanced around it.

The room was not very large, but attractively decorated in soft blue and cream. Over the fireplace hung a portrait of Simon's parents.

"It just doesn't seem right to put them in one of the guest rooms," Mrs. Bradford went on. "Simon should not feel like a guest in his own home."

Madeline slipped her arm through Mrs. Bradford's and hugged her close. "Don't you think it would be wise to wait until you've met his wife?" she cautioned quietly. "I mean, I am certain she will be wonderful in every way, but suppose she was not—" She paused slightly. "You know, Simon was away a long time and must have been very lonely. When he found someone whose company he enjoyed, he might have been willing to overlook certain things."

"He wouldn't marry someone unsuitable."

"Let's just wait to see, shall we?" Madeline suggested pleasantly. "Giving them the smaller bedroom first will hurt no one. And if she turns out to be all that we hope, you can still give them everything you want."

"I suppose you are right." Mrs. Bradford patted Madeline's hand fondly. "You are always the practical one. I am lucky that Nigel married you."

Madeline smiled humbly but said nothing.

"Why don't you wait downstairs?" Mrs. Bradford suggested. "I shall be down in a moment."

As the older woman went down the hall to her own room, Madeline slowly descended the stairs. Nigel was waiting at the bottom.

"She all set for the grand homecoming?" he asked as he checked his appearance in the large mirror on the wall.

Madeline watched him fussing first with his cravat, then his hair. "She's ready to fall all over them," she whispered. "And all you care about is your fool hair. Don't you find anything slightly havey-cavey about this whole affair?"

"Such as?" Nigel's smile was elegant unconcern.

68

"Such as the fact that Simon never mentioned a wife in his letters. Never mentioned her at all, to be honest, until Grandmother did," Madeline pointed out. "Does that sound normal to you?"

"Sounds like Simon. He never did things the way everyone else did."

A noise from upstairs startled Madeline, but a quick glance assured her Mrs. Bradford wasn't coming down yet. "Don't you care what's happening?" Madeline groused. "Do you want to hand everything over to Simon just because he has decided to come home? You have just as much right to the estate as he does."

Nigel turned back to the mirror. "That is quite true. There was no entail, so I could inherit through my mother just as easily as he could inherit through his father, but what you seem intent on forgetting, my dear, is that there is nothing to inherit until Grandmother dies."

"You can hardly wait until she does to secure your interest," Madeline pointed out. "You cannot sit back and let Simon waltz off with everything. We need to fight back."

He just laughed. "My dear girl, Simon has been in favor before, but he never manages to retain it very long. Grandmother is pleased to see him, but that is only because in the three years he was gone, she has managed to forget just how irresponsible he is. I do not think we need do anything but sit back and watch. Simon will throw away his inheritance himself."

Madeline was not convinced, but Mrs. Bradford was coming down the stairs, so she turned to smile up at her.

"I thought I heard a carriage stop in front of the house. Do you think it could be them?" Mrs. Bradford asked.

"Perhaps we should rush out to the street to see?"

Nigel's suggestion was sarcastic, but Mrs. Bradford looked half tempted by the idea. Then she shook her head regretfully. "No, we had best wait in the drawing room."

Catherine waited as Simon climbed from the carriage, then he reached up to take Teddy from her arms. The house before them looked cold and imposing, sending a shiver down her spine. Everything would be fine, she told herself for the hundredth time that day, and let Simon help her out of the carriage. She had Simon now, she whispered to her soul, she wasn't alone anymore.

"You mustn't worry so," Simon told her quietly as the coachmen began to unload their things. "Grandmother and Madeline will become your best friends."

Catherine just smiled rather thinly at him. "Are my worries that obvious? Here I thought no one but me was aware of the butterflies that must have snuck into my breakfast." She wished she had the courage to ask him how he felt about living in the same house as Madeline and her husband, but she just clutched Teddy while the house frowned at her with haughty disapproval.

"If I remember correctly, your breakfast plate was sent back untouched, so you can't blame what you

70

ate."

"I guess not." This time she did manage a smile for him and, once he was satisfied that none of their luggage was likely to be left on the coach, he took her arm and led her up the stairs to the front door.

The panic in her stomach increased with each step she took. "Didn't you say you had a sister?" Catherine asked, grasping for anything to distract her from her fears. "Does she live here too?"

"Anne? Yes, she does, but she is away. Though you need not worry about her either."

Before he could say any more, the front door had opened and the old butler stood there, smiling at them.

"Have the luggage brought in, will you, Benson?" Simon asked. He gave Catherine a comforting squeeze as he led her into the house.

With a deep breath Catherine looked around her. The foyer did not seem any more welcoming than the outside of the house. The floor was cool white stone while the walls were a deep green color. The stairway in the center of the room was carpeted in dark red, its posts and handrail carved ornately in some dark wood. The only cheerful spot in the room was a small bowl of white flowers on a table off to one side. A sense of welcome didn't matter, she told herself, she and Simon were married. There was nothing the others could do about that.

"The family is in the drawing room. Shall I announce you?" the butler asked quietly.

"No, we shall go up ourselves," Simon said, leading Catherine up the stairs.

But what if Simon changed his mind about her? What was the saying? Marry in haste, repent in leisure. Was that what Simon would do?

The upper hall was slightly more cheerful, but it did little to still the tremors in Catherine's soul. Several bowls of flowers were around, and, although the dark red carpeting was up there also, the walls were a pale gold. Portraits were on the wall along the stairs, and they seemed to be watching her kindly. She tried to take courage from them.

"Remember to be careful what you say," Simon cautioned her quietly. "Do not let on that we were just married today."

Her smile faded as a hundred questions bombarded her mind. There was so much they hadn't discussed, so much they hadn't even thought to cover. How much of her life was she allowed to reveal? Could she admit that she had been married before? And what about Teddy? In the rush of the last few hours, she had never thought to ask Simon.

"Simon!" she cried, grabbing his sleeve in panic just as he was about to open the drawing room door.

He stopped and looked at her questioningly.

"Simon, what about Teddy?" she whispered. The baby had somehow managed to get the ruff around her neck in his hand, and was happily tugging it. She gently tried to loosen his grip as Simon took her arm.

"He will be fine," he said, misunderstanding her question. He pushed open the drawing room door just as Teddy, deprived of his ruff, let out a piercing scream.

For a long moment no one but Teddy said anything. Catherine tried frantically to quiet him, but he must have sensed her sudden panic, for he just would not be silenced.

Suddenly, there was a large, elderly woman in a pale rose dress standing right in front of Catherine. "Oh, Simon," she sighed loudly, and threw her arms around an astonished Catherine and Teddy. She released them after a moment, tears streaming down her cheeks. "Oh, Simon, why didn't you tell us?"

Simon put his arm around Catherine again. "Grandmother, this is Catherine, and that"—he pointed to the still-screaming infant—"is Teddy."

"He is beautiful," the woman cried with an uncertain smile for Catherine. "May I hold him?"

Without a word Catherine gave Teddy to her. Mrs. Bradford held him gently, as if he were the most precious thing in the whole world, and Catherine's heart sank. How could she ever tell Simon's grandmother that Teddy was from another marriage?

In the midst of his crying Teddy's hand brushed against a button on Mrs. Bradford's dress. His little fingers closed around it tightly, and his crying stopped immediately. Mrs. Bradford smiled down at him, then held out her hand to Catherine.

"Why, Simon, she is no more than a child herself," she scolded.

"I hardly snatched her from the nursery," he laughed.

Mrs. Bradford shook her head, and led Catherine across the room. "You don't look more than sixteen," she said. "Certainly not old enough to be a wife and mother."

"Actually, I'm twenty."

"You see, Grandmother, she is practically ancient," Simon pointed out as Mrs. Bradford led her over to the others in the room.

"This is some more of Simon's family. His cousin, Nigel, and Nigel's wife, Madeline. I imagine Simon mentioned them."

"Yes, of course, Simon has told me all about them," Catherine said lightly, but her smile dimmed as she gazed at Madeline.

Nigel's wife was as beautiful as Catherine had feared she would be. She was tall and regal-looking, with dark brown hair that was arranged in an elegant style. Even the black dress she was wearing was the very essence of style and good taste. Catherine felt very provincial.

"How wonderful to meet you," Madeline purred though her eyes stayed cold and hard. "Simon was so mysterious about you that we began to wonder just what you were like."

Catherine read the challenge in her voice. "That's Simon," she laughed, and patted Simon's arm in what she hoped was a fond manner. Simon, however, seemed hardly aware of her. He was looking at Madeline, his lips tightly compressed as he evidently fought to keep his love for her from showing.

Catherine sighed and allowed Mrs. Bradford to show her to a spot on a settee. Madeline and Nigel sat across from them, while Simon moved a chair close to his grandmother's side.

"Would you like me to take Teddy?" Catherine offered as a footman brought in tea. She felt more alone, more vulnerable without Teddy in her arms.

"No, you may not," Mrs. Bradford laughed. "He is quite happy where he is and so am I."

Catherine smiled weakly and watched as Madeline poured tea.

"It must be quite exciting for you to be in London," Madeline said to Catherine as she passed a cup across to her. "I imagine that you have never seen anything like it."

Catherine smiled back. Was that really condescension in Madeline's voice, Catherine wondered, or was she being too sensitive, wanting to find fault with Simon's love? "I'm afraid that it doesn't seem much different from Boston or Halifax," she said carefully. "Just older." She picked up her cup, stirring the tea slowly. Don't see problems where there are none, she scolded herself. Don't decide that Madeline has to be your enemy because Simon loves her.

"Halifax?" Madeline asked as she passed cups to Simon and Nigel. "Have you been there?"

Mrs. Bradford looked up from playing with Teddy. "Edward was in Halifax, was he not?"

Catherine's heart froze. "Edward?" Her voice sounded weak and lost, and she tried again. "Who is Edward?" It couldn't be him; it couldn't be.

"Madeline's brother," Simon explained. He leaned forward to pick up Catherine's spoon which she hadn't been aware of dropping, then helped himself to a small lemon cake.

"Oh." Catherine put the spoon on the saucer carefully. She shouldn't be so silly. There must have been any number of Edwards in Halifax in the past few years.

"It was so tragic," Mrs. Bradford told her. "He was killed around the same time Simon was wounded, and we shall all miss him."

"How sad." There was no connection between this Edward and her husband. It was just a coincidence. But her hand continued to echo the trembling of her heart, and she thought it best to put her cup down on the table until she could convince herself to relax.

"We must have a party to introduce Catherine to our friends," Mrs. Bradford said. "Everyone will be so eager to meet her once they hear Simon has married."

"A party would be wonderful," Simon agreed. "It would give me a chance to renew some old acquaintances too."

"It will have to be small," his grandmother went on. "Madeline is still in mourning, but we could seat about twenty for dinner and maybe another ten or so later." She turned to Catherine. "Have you any friends or relations here in London that you would like to invite?"

"No, I'm afraid I know no one here but you people." Her hands steady once more, she reached for her cup. Edward was a common name. She couldn't have an attack of the vapors each time she heard it. She was going to have to get stronger.

"That will soon change. In no time you'll be in such demand that we'll never see you." Mrs. Bradford turned to Madeline. "Do you think your parents would come? Or are they still in the country?"

"Mother is not here, but I do believe that Father

and Michael are both in town. Though I could not say if they would come, being in mourning also."

"I am certain that they will be eager to meet Catherine," Mrs. Bradford said. "I think we can safely count on Lord Killian and Michael attending. Now, who else can we invite?"

Lord Killian! Catherine's heart stopped. No! It couldn't be! Fate couldn't be that cruel, or could it?

Horror clutching at her breath, Catherine's shocked gaze went from Madeline to Nigel to Simon and his grandmother, but they were all chatting about the party and paying her no mind. It could not be the same Lord Killian, could it? But even as she hoped it wasn't, she knew it was. Fate had not been on her side since she met Edward. Meeting Simon had only been its way of teasing her into relaxing before this gigantic blow. And now their lie of a marriage would be exposed as a fraud and Simon would be disgraced.

As she watched numbly, her cup slipped from her lifeless fingers and fell to the floor. It shattered, just as the peace she had hoped to have would, but the sound finally freed her from the paralysis and she leapt to her feet.

"I am dreadfully sorry," she cried as she tried to gather up the broken pieces. "It just slipped from my hand."

"Oh, don't touch it. You'll cut yourself," Mrs. Bradford said quickly as Simon rang for a footman to clean up the broken china. "You aren't hurt, are you? You look so pale."

"No, I am fine. Just a little clumsy, I fear." Catherine sat back down, clutching her hands together to keep them from trembling noticeably. What was she to do? Everyone was being so kind, so loving. How could she allow her presence to bring them ridicule?

Madeline smiled at her. "I think it was my father's name that sent her into a panic."

Catherine's breath caught for a moment, but she forced herself to look directly at Madeline. Was the time already here for exposure? Maybe it would be better this way.

Madeline's smile broadened, but not altogether pleasantly. "Perhaps the idea of meeting nobility is a little frightening to someone from the colonies," she said. "I do not suppose you have met an actual duke or lord before, have you?"

Relief washed over Catherine like a cleansing wave, leaving her exhausted but strangely refreshed. "No, I have not," she admitted readily. Let them believe she was provincial or one step above a savage, she no longer cared as long as they did not know the real truth just yet. She needed time to think things through, something she should have done before she married Simon that morning. She was grateful when Teddy began to fuss.

"He must be tired," she said, and took him from Mrs. Bradford's arms. "The trip has been hard on us both."

Mrs. Bradford stood up. "We shall have to get a nursery set up for him and find him a nanny."

"I do not mind taking care of him," Catherine said. It didn't seem right for Simon's family to do so much for her and Teddy.

"But you must have help. You will wear yourself

78

out otherwise," Mrs. Bradford told her. "Let me show you to your room now."

Catherine was glad that Simon had risen to his feet also and was preparing to come with them. It was going to be impossibly difficult, but she was going to have to tell him about Edward.

Mrs. Bradford had other plans though. "Simon, go tell Benson all the things you will need for the nursery, so we can set it up as soon as possible. I am certain Catherine can do without you for a little while."

Simon went off to find the butler while Catherine followed Mrs. Bradford to their room. The house seemed less cold and forbidding, but now a prison of a different sort.

Michael Corbett-Smith was leaving the house when Lord Killian opened the door of his library. "Ah, Michael, just the person I wanted to see," he called out as if it had been an accidental meeting, not one his lordship had been planning for days. "Do come in for a few minutes, will you?" He stepped aside from the door, but Michael stayed where he was in the hallway.

"Come now, Michael, surely you can spare a few moments of your time for your father?" he asked, his voice a little sharper this time.

Michael sighed and reluctantly followed his father into the room. He sank into a chair before the desk and leaned back, looking bored.

Lord Killian noted Michael's appearance and attitude, but said nothing though his lips tightened slightly as he walked over to the liquor cabinet. "Would you like something? A glass of Madeira, perhaps?"

"All right," Michael grudgingly agreed.

His father poured out the glasses, and carried them over to where his son sat. He carefully handed one to him and then sat on the edge of his desk, holding on to his own glass. He took a small sip, then put the glass down next to him.

"I would like you to come to Tattersalls with me tomorrow morning," he announced.

Michael's eyebrows rose. "Why? We have all the horses we need already. There is barely enough exercise for them around the estate as it is."

"No, I am not thinking of the estate," Lord Killian said. He took another sip of his wine, swallowing his impatience along with it. Handling Michael was not unlike breaking a stallion. Persistence and strength were needed. "I have heard there is an exceptionally fine matched set of four blacks for sale. I thought you might enjoy them."

"What would I do with four horses in London?" Michael asked impatiently. "Riding requires only one horse, and driving two. Does not four seem a trifle too many?"

"Four is not too many for some people to handle," his father snapped. "And since you have no desire to join Prinny's inner circle, and have made almost no use of your memberships at Whites and Brooks, I was merely trying to find some aspect of society that might interest you."

Michael stood up, putting his half-empty glass down on his father's desk. "So you decided I ought to join the Four-in-Hand Club?" he asked, sounding disgusted. "I hate to keep repeating myself, Father, but I have no interest in any of the affectations of society. I have better things to do with my time than to try to amuse a fat, gouty old man, or throw away good money during a boring card game. Although I do enjoy my horses, driving four through the streets of London, for no better reason than to prove my skill or win a bet, seems the height of folly. Why can you not just accept the fact that I am not Edward, and let me choose my own interests?"

Michael turned toward the door, not waiting for an answer, but Lord Killian's anger burst into action. He was on his feet in a flash, calling after his son, "You must start taking part in society! You are my heir!"

Michael turned at the door. "I wish to God I were not. I wish that Edward had married and left an heir! I would gladly pass up all the glory for a little peace!" The door closed quite solidly behind him.

For a long moment Lord Killian stared at the closed door without really seeing it as Michael's words echoed in his mind. Edward left an heir. Edward left an heir.

Lord Killian walked slowly over to his desk, remembering that conniving woman who had claimed to have been married to Edward. Of course, she hadn't been. He knew Edward too well to believe that he would choose some drab from the stews to bear the Killian children, but supposing she took those marriage lines to a lawyer? Would they be recognized for the false bit of nonsense that they were, or would she be able to make trouble? Would her brat be recognized as Edward's heir?

Throughout his whole life Lord Killian had been careful to avoid any hint of scandal, yet now some impudent hussy could ruin all for him. He turned to the window and stared blindly at the carriages below him. He had to get those marriage lines back. Without them, her story would just be dismissed as lies. But with that paper there was no telling who might believe her ridiculous tale. He should never have allowed her to leave with them.

Filled with sudden decision, Lord Killian strode quickly from the room, grabbing his hat and walking stick from the butler and hurrying out of the house. After walking briskly for the next half hour, he left the wealthier part of London. He went through dirty streets littered with rotting garbage and past half-naked children and whining beggars, but his pace did not change. Disgust was the only emotion stirring his blood. Disgust and determination to do what was needed to protect Edward's memory.

Lord Killian finally reached an inn named The Oxbow and, pushing open the door, he stepped into the dark interior that reeked from the smell of rotting food and unwashed bodies. A wave of nausea was quickly swallowed; he was in control, tightly reined and not subject to the weakness of lesser men. After a moment to let his eyes adjust to the darkened room, he walked over to a man in a far corner and sat down across from him.

The man was thin with a scraggly gray beard and leaned back against the wall as he drank a tankard of ale. He did not move when Lord Killian joined him, his face expressionless.

"I have a job for you," Lord Killian said quietly.

The man leaned forward and glanced around the inn, but no one was near them. "What?" the man asked.

"I want a certain woman found," Lord Killian told him. "I know little about her, except that she goes by the name of Catherine Smith. She came from Canada very recently, probably in the last week. She's small and thin, and not more than twenty years old. When I saw her, she was dressed in some cheap black dress that was supposed to pass for mourning clothes."

"And when I find 'er?" the man asked.

"I want a piece of paper she has," Lord Killian explained.

The man drained his tankard. "I'm ta find this woman jest fer a piece of paper? What's on it?"

Lord Killian's face became closed and forbidding. "It hardly matters what is on it," he snapped. "I will pay you well to get it, that is all that concerns you."

The man shrugged and leaned negligently back against the wall again. "And 'ow am I to know which paper is the one ya want?"

"The one I want is fairly worn, and has been folded. It is about this big"—Lord Killian indicated the size with his hands—"and has writing in black ink on one side. Although it is not of any real importance, it does look rather official."

The man smiled unpleasantly in obvious disbelief of the worthlessness of this paper, but Lord Killian

83

cared not. The man was being hired for a job he was qualified to do and that was all.

"And is the woman alone?" the man asked.

"She may have a baby with her," Lord Killian said.

The man shook his head. "I meant someone who might give me trouble."

But Lord Killian only shrugged. "I do not know of anyone, but it might be possible."

The man leaned forward suddenly, putting his elbows on the table and bringing his face very close to Lord Killian's. "It will cost ya a century," he whispered.

"Do not be a fool, man," Lord Killian snapped. "I am willing to pay fifty pounds, but no more than that."

"Seventy then."

"But only if you get that paper before anyone else sees it," Lord Killian warned as he stood up. "If I even hear a hint of rumor about it, I will not pay a cent." He picked up his hat from the table. "I will come here a week from today at this time. Have the paper."

Chapter Five

The door was barely closed behind Mrs. Bradford and Catherine when Madeline flew to her feet and confronted Nigel. "Do you still think we can just sit back and wait for Simon to ruin things for himself?" she cried. Her hands tried to wring the grief and worry from her being, but seemed only to make her agitation grow as she saw again in her memory the warmth in Mrs. Bradford's eyes and heard the soft fondness in her voice.

"My God," Madeline said. "I thought she was going to sign the estate over to them during tea."

Nigel was the picture of serenity: his face relaxed, his movements calm as a spectator with nothing wagered on a horse race. "My dear, what is there to get upset about?" he asked. "So things went well today. They may not tomorrow. The charming bride did have a tendency to be rather clumsy."

Why couldn't he see the truth? Madeline wondered. "The little bride has also produced a great-grandchild, you may have noticed. I think that will more than outweigh any slight clumsiness she has."

Madeline paced back and forth for a few minutes, too restless, too determined to sit still and wait for defeat. She spun around suddenly to frown at Nigel. "I refuse to stand by and watch our home be given away from us."

His smile was faintly amused though his voice held just the hint of steel. "And I thought you married me for love, not my expectations." He lay his arm along the back of the brocade-covered settee, his fingers idly tracing over the cabbage-flower design. "Might I ask just how you intend to fight them? Are you going to have a baby too?"

Madeline glared at his flippancy and turned away, clutching the back of a chair thoughtfully. "Since it seems impossible for me to produce the first great-grandchild, I think I shall try some other method."

"I thought you might."

She flung him an angry glance, quite irritated with his refusal to see the danger in Simon's presence. Why couldn't she have found a man with backbone, someone like her father or Edward? They would not have left her to fight her battles alone. "If you really want to know, I shall become darling Catherine's dearest friend. I shall win her confidence and worm all the secrets out of her until I find something I can use."

"My, how delightful! The perfect friend."

But Madeline refused to be goaded any further. She was doing what had to be done and Nigel's mockery would not turn her aside. "Laugh if you like, but when I turn your grandmother against them, you won't be so smug."

"Probably not, although your schemes often seem to go awry." He rose languidly to his feet. "I hope you won't be offended, but all this intrigue does tire me out so. I think I shall go down to Whites for a few hours."

"Nigel," Madeline called, and hurried to meet him at the door. "I may need your help."

His eyebrows rose delicately. "Am I also to be a confidant, the wormer of secrets?"

What was the matter with him lately? Had he no pride? "This is important to our future. You have to help me."

"Ah, yes, I remember now. It was in the wedding vows after love and honor, wasn't it? I promised to love, honor, and help you with your devious schemes." His smile was more bitter than fond. "Funny how the things you promise at your wedding seem to slip so easily from your mind, isn't it?" He was gone before Madeline's angry retort left her lips.

She clamped her mouth shut, refusing to give in to the childish impulse to shout her answer after him. What did it matter? She could do very well without his help.

She would find a way to ensure that Bradleigh was not lost to her forever, regardless of Nigel's strange moods. She would do it for her father. When she had Bradleigh in her control, then her father would approve of her, then he would respect her. His daughter, a mere female, would have given him his fondest dream, something even Edward had not been able to do.

Madeline had been fourteen when she had first

87

heard the story. A hundred years earlier, an unscrupulous Bradford had taken advantage of the financial difficulties of the current Lord Killian, purchasing a large portion of the estate that had not been entailed. He even had the audacity to enlarge an old guest house on the property into his family home!

But the property was still rightfully part of the Killian estate, and for years Madeline's father had been striving determinedly to get it back. His repeated offers to purchase it had been refused, and though he had ceased to mention it, Madeline knew his fervor had not eased. Shackled though he might be by laws, Madeline had known even at fourteen how she could get it for him: All she had to do was marry the heir, then convince him to sell it to her father. How could she not win his favor then?

What could go wrong with her plan when Simon, obviously his grandmother's favorite and therefore heir, had been ready to die for a smile from her lips? When he sighed and swooned with love when she spoke his name? Unwittingly, her father had botched her whole plan in thwarting their elopement and forcing Simon's enlistment into the army.

She had fretted and fumed with uncertainty. How could she hold Simon's interest when he was so far away? Maybe she needn't, she had realized suddenly, seeing how dependent Mrs. Bradford was becoming on Nigel. She married him quickly when they learned of Simon's grave injury the year before, for fear that Simon's death would force Nigel into mourning and they would have to wait a year. Instead, it was Edward's death that sent her into mourning.

Still, she could feel Bradleigh within her grasp and hadn't even worried when the expected news of Simon's death had never come. She had worked hard to endear herself to Mrs. Bradford, never losing an opportunity to point out to her just how dependable Nigel was and how well he was running her estate. Even Simon's return bothered her little. He was still obviously devoted to her, in spite of his marriage.

It was that squawling infant that had changed everything, that put all she had worked for in danger. But success would not be snatched away by some little nobody from Canada. Bradleigh was going to be her father's, and Madeline would not let anyone stand in her way.

"Do you mind if I stay?" Mrs. Bradford asked.

Catherine looked up from the bed where she had lain Teddy, trying not to let her weariness creep into her voice. "No, of course not." But how she longed for a moment alone, some time to think and plan what she was to do! She felt as if she'd hardly been able to breathe since she came through that front door, and not at all since she'd learned Edward was Madeline's brother. What was she to do?

"I would not be offended if you preferred to be alone."

"No, really. Stay." How could she refuse the eagerness in Mrs. Bradford's voice, the loneliness in her eyes? Being alone with Teddy would serve no purpose but give Catherine more time to fret. The first chance she had she must tell Simon, that was all. He had to know, and maybe, just maybe, he would keep her safe.

Catherine bent over Teddy to take off the little sweater she'd knitted him after Edward's death, trying not to remember her fears then. She wasn't alone anymore, she had Simon now. He didn't love her, but he was kind. And she hadn't done anything to be ashamed of. The situation was awkward certainly, but not desperate. A maid brought up some warm water, and Mrs. Bradford had her put it in the washbasin, then shooed her back out the door.

"I did not think we needed her help," Mrs. Bradford said. She leaned over Teddy, and gently tickled his cheek. His laughter was reflected in her face.

When the news about her marriage to Edward came out, the truth about Teddy would also, Catherine realized. Why hadn't they thought about that? Was she being foolish to think Simon would stand by her? She had known the marriage was a foolhardy step to take. Why had she allowed him to persuade her? Why had she let the warmth of his smile befuddle her mind?

Teddy's needs were more immediate than her worries though, and she took comfort from caring for him. She washed him and changed him into clean clothes, not allowing herself to ache for Simon's grandmother as she fussed over the baby.

"He's such a little darling," Mrs. Bradford sighed. "When is his birthday?"

Catherine had been unbuttoning the front of her dress. "January seventh," she said absently, and slipped her dress off one shoulder to unfasten the zona that supported her breasts.

"Oh, that must have been a terrible time for you."

Catherine glanced up. It had been but how would Mrs. Bradford know that?

"With Simon still so ill and all," the older woman went on. "We certainly owe you a great deal. I cannot imagine too many women in your condition who would have been able to nurse their husbands back to health. Why, I do not believe I was out of the house the last four months before I gave birth to Simon's father."

Catherine brushed aside Mrs. Bradford's words. "It was not that uncommon at home to see women about right up to the time of their confinement."

"And I imagine Simon's needs would override any embarrassment you might feel about your size or awkwardness." Seeing Catherine was ready to nurse, Mrs. Bradford picked up Teddy from the bed. "Where are you going to sit?"

"I think here in the sun," Catherine said, pointing to a comfortable-looking chair in a patch of sunlight. "We'll both stay warm."

"I could have a fire made," the other woman offered.

"No, we'll be fine."

She settled into the chair with Teddy, relaxing as he took her breast. So much had changed in the few months since he was born, yet he was unaffected by it all. He trusted her, and feeling the rush of love that always came when she held him close, she vowed never to betray that trust. She was strong enough to keep that vow.

"I cannot tell you how happy I am that Simon married you," Mrs. Bradford said suddenly, dragging Catherine's eyes from her son. "Did he tell you about Madeline?"

That was not a topic Catherine particularly wanted to pursue, but the magic spell between her and Teddy was broken anyway. "Yes," she admitted. "I knew about her."

Mrs. Bradford seemed relieved. "I know that at one time he thought he was in love with her, but he wasn't. Not really. The only reason they eloped was because he was so impulsive."

Teddy's quiet murmurings had been drawing Catherine's attention back to him, but Mrs. Bradford's words called it back. "They eloped?"

"Oh, dear." The kindly woman looked upset. "I thought you said you knew about her."

"I thought I did." She had known Simon loved Madeline. Why should the fact they had eloped make it much more serious? The warm sun streaming in had no effect on her. A chill had seeped in, stealing the caress from the sun's touch.

"Not that it matters now," Mrs. Bradford assured her. "That was absolutely ages ago. Since he married you, it is obvious that his feelings for her are all gone."

Was it? Not if one knew the real story of their marriage. "What happened?" she asked, knowing she didn't really want to know. "When they eloped, I mean."

Mrs. Bradford shrugged. "Nothing, really. Madeline's father caught up with them before they got very far. Everything was hushed up and Simon

92

joined the army. It seems to have been just the thing for him, for he appears to have become quite responsible."

But the results of Simon's military career were not uppermost in Catherine's mind. To have eloped, Simon must have felt very deeply about Madeline. And she must have returned his feelings. To risk censure and scandal just to be with the one you loved, that was not the results of a mild fondness. No wonder Simon expected Madeline would be waiting for him.

"Madeline must have missed him terribly when he was gone," Catherine said.

"Oh, I doubt that," Mrs. Bradford said. "She's not emotional like Simon. She agreed to that elopement for her own reasons, what they were I do not know, but they were not love. Perhaps she was piqued with her father or thought it would be a highly romantic thing to do. Whatever it was, I thank God they were stopped. It would have been a disastrous marriage."

"Yet she married your other grandson," Catherine pointed out.

"That was different." Mrs. Bradford waved her hand. "Nigel can take care of himself, and he knew Madeline for what she was: lovely to look at and amusing, but not one to offer love. Simon would have broken his heart trying to please her, and never would have succeeded. He's the type to love totally, without reservation, and Madeline is not capable of love like that."

From all she had heard of Madeline, and the little Catherine had seen of her, she was inclined to agree. But she could not convince herself that Simon was free of Madeline's spell. Yet while he still cared for his cousin's wife, what kind of a marriage could she and Simon have together?

"Now, you must not be upset," Mrs. Bradford said. Catherine's thoughts obviously were mirrored on her face. "I would never have mentioned it if I thought you did not already know. You are the one Simon loves now and you are the one he married. Forget about Madeline."

If only Catherine could! But Teddy once again reclaimed her attention, and brought her back down to reality. So what if Simon loved another? He had not promised her love, just security, and he would be true to his word. He was giving her and Teddy a badly needed home. Love was not part of their bargain. She had had her chance at love with Edward. He had been devoted when they first married and it had quickly changed. Perhaps she was not the type to inspire lasting love. She must learn to live without it.

The portrait of a young couple and a young boy above the fireplace caught Catherine's eye and provided a diversion from her melancholy thoughts. "Are those Simon's parents?" she asked, for the man looked astonishingly like Simon.

Mrs. Bradford looked up at the portrait also with the fond vague smile of someone slipping into happier memories. "Yes. That was painted when Simon was about three."

Catherine studied the picture more intently. "He rarely mentions his parents."

"No, I do not suppose he would. He was very

young when they died, and Anne was just an infant."

"Then they came to live with you?"

Mrs. Bradford's gaze shifted as she saw days from the past. "And it was quite an experience, let me tell you. They hadn't a penny between them and precious little sense either. But we managed."

Catherine could see the love the older woman had for Simon and remembered the affection with which he had spoken of her. "He feels very close to you also."

Mrs. Bradford returned to the present and nodded as a knock was heard at the door. She got to her feet, opening it carefully to shelter Catherine from prying eyes. "It's only Simon," she said, and let him in.

"We found a cradle in the attic," he said, then stopped short at the sight of Catherine nursing.

She stared back at him, a mixture of embarrassment and concern. Would he say something that would expose their hasty marriage?

"Oh, excuse me," he mumbled, and took a step back toward the door.

"Don't be silly," his grandmother laughed. "It's not as if this is the first time you've seen Catherine nursing the baby."

"No, no, of course not." But his unwavering gaze brought a blush to Catherine's cheeks. She felt as if he were seeing her for the first time and turned her own eyes onto Teddy. She sensed that Simon turned aside. "Where do you want the cradle?" he asked his grandmother.

"I think the end bedroom would be best for the

nursery, but until we get someone in to care for the baby, I think the cradle will have to go in here."

Catherine looked up at that. "In here? But that will disturb Simon's sleep. Would it not be better if I slept in the nursery?"

"Heavens, no." Mrs. Bradford was firm. "The room needs a good cleaning and airing. It'll be much easier to have the little sweetheart in here for now, but I will get the maids started on fixing up the nursery." She left them alone together.

Simon was silent for a moment after the door closed, then cleared his throat. "I'm sorry about barging in like that, but I thought it would look odd if I rushed back out. Besides," he added with a soft smile. "It was such a lovely scene, I did not wish to leave it."

Catherine felt her cheeks burn, but smiled shyly up at him. Her husband was a very handsome man, she realized not for the first time. His hair was a soft brown, his eyes a darker shade that could light with laughter. He was tall and broad-shouldered with an aura of strength and protection about him. Her breath quickened; the load of worries on her heart seemed less. She could learn to care about Simon very easily, she realized, but would that be the type of relationship he'd want?

"I'm sorry about Teddy having to sleep in here," she said.

Simon moved closer across the room—their room—and sat on their bed. The fire in her cheeks felt even hotter, the room smaller, for Simon seemed to be everywhere she looked. Or was it just that her eyes seemed unable to look anywhere but at him?

"Actually, I had already planned to sleep in the dressing room next door for the next several nights," he said. "I thought it would give us more time to get to know each other. I know I rushed you into the marriage and would like to let you relax."

She was not certain she wanted such consideration. "I knew what I was doing when I married you," she pointed out.

He seemed to find that amusing, as well he might. She hadn't exactly done much but follow along with his every suggestion.

"I seem to remember bullying you shamelessly," he said. "And giving you no opportunity to refuse."

"You make me sound very lily-livered."

"Not at all." He leaned closer, close enough to pat her knee gently and awaken in her a longing to be held, to lie close in the safety of his arms and find peace. "I think you have a great deal of courage. You survived the death of your father and your husband and still had the strength to come to this country. But now that your worries are over, I want you to have time to relax."

Her worries over! His words were enough to bring them all back. "Simon—" She leaned forward, jostling Teddy slightly but enough to make him lose her breast and begin to complain. That and her partially naked body drove all thought of speech from her. She could not tell him about Edward, sitting here as she was.

He got to his feet. "I shall see what they are doing with the cradle. I do not know much about babies, but surely Teddy ought to be getting tired soon."

97

She nodded and let him leave, still unaware that their hasty marriage was certain to be disclosed soon. But once she got Teddy settled, she would seek him out and tell him. She would not let the day end without Simon knowing the truth.

Yet, the chance to tell Simon seemed unwilling to present itself. The afternoon passed into evening without them having a moment alone together. Then they'd all dined and were now in the drawing room.

"We shall have to visit all the best mantilla-makers before we schedule the party," Mrs. Bradford was saying.

"I shall take her shopping with me," Madeline announced. Catherine glanced up, startled almost out of her fretting as Madeline went on. "We can go out tomorrow morning and order everything she needs. It will be such fun."

The other woman's smile held such warmth and friendliness that it caught Catherine off guard. Had she misjudged Simon's former love? Had she been jealous of his devotion to Madeline and mean-spiritedly refused to see she was kind?

"Thank you. I appreciate your help," Catherine said slowly.

Madeline's eyes reflected nothing but pleasure. "I can tell we shall be such friends."

Nigel raised his glass of brandy in toastlike fashion. "Ah, to the joys of true friendship."

Strangely enough, Madeline tossed him a frosty glance, then turned back solicitously to Catherine.

"You must tell me all about your home in Canada."

It seemed an innocent question accompanied by an innocent smile, but it brought Catherine's panic back. What had Simon already told them? Had he written to them much with details of his life? Before she could stammer out an answer though, a commotion was heard out in the hallway and a young woman dressed in black swooped into the room. She was tall and slender, with hair the color of Simon's.

"I thought we would never get home," she cried, and threw herself into the nearest chair. "First, the carriage—" She stopped and sat up, her face alight with pleasure. "Simon!"

Simon barely had time to get to his feet before the young woman had thrown herself into his arms. "How marvelous to see you! Why did you not let me know you were coming? I would never have gone to Bath."

"There is a great deal Simon neglected to tell us, Anne," Mrs. Bradford said with a laugh. She rose to her feet and pulled Catherine to hers. "This is his wife, Catherine."

Anne's infectious joy captured Catherine in a hug which she returned with equal fervor. There was nothing pretentious about Simon's sister. She was warm and welcoming.

"This is wonderful!" Anne cried, her eyes brimming over with happy tears. "And to think the Johnstones actually wanted me to stay another week in Bath when there was such excitement here!"

"I fully share your enthusiasm, Anne," Nigel said in a voice that barely sounded alive, let alone thrilled. "But could you not contain it until you removed some of the dirt of traveling?"

Anne only laughed, taking Nigel's reprimands lightly. "I do beg your pardon," she said with a deep curtsy in his direction that showed off her rumpled traveling dress. "I fear some of this dust may be from Bath, and we all know that is not up to London's standards." She straightened up and headed toward the door. "I shall remove all offending traces."

"Anne!" Simon stopped his sister at the door, his hand a loving support on her arm. "Anne, I was so sorry to hear about Edward."

Catherine caught her breath as she saw Anne's smile dim. It still was curving her lips upward, but had no reflection in her eyes.

"I would rather not talk about it," Anne said softly. Her voice quivered with emotion and her eyes filled with tears.

Catherine felt as if she were intruding just by watching, and turned away, strolling over to where Nigel stood at the liquor cabinet.

"Is the Edward that Simon mentioned to Anne Madeline's brother?" Catherine asked. "I don't mean to pry, but it seems to have upset her so . . ."

Nigel's eyes followed hers to Simon, and Anne still standing in the doorway. Anne had gone from a laughing young woman to a figure of depression and unhappiness in just the space of a few words. Her shoulders were slumped and her hand was clinging to Simon's.

"Yes, that was Madeline's brother," Nigel said quietly. For once his voice was quiet without the tinge of sarcasm that always seemed to flavor it. "He and Anne were betrothed."

"Betrothed?" It was a gasp of disbelief, of pain and despair. "Anne and Edward?"

Nigel's eyes came back to her, cynicism masking any other emotion they might have betrayed. "Yes, our Anne and the perfect Edward. It was an unlikely match."

There was something in his voice that made her warm to him, as if she had found an unexpected ally. "You sound as if you did not like Edward."

He took a sip of his brandy. "Not like Edward?" His smile was not pleasant. "How could anyone not like the saintly Edward? He excelled at everything — horses, cards, women. His manners were perfect and his taste impeccable. Oh, no, we all loved him dearly, little cousin-in-law, and we must all worship at his throne daily."

With that remark hanging in the air, he wandered across the room to sit down next to Madeline. Catherine's eyes were drawn back to Anne and Simon still in quiet conversation at the door. How alike they were in appearance, even down to the sharing of grief. How would Simon feel when he learned that his wife had been married to his sister's fiancé? How could she tell him?

Chapter Six

A sleepless night of tossing and turning and endless vacillating finally brought Catherine around to
a decision about the same time the dawn brought
light to the sky. There was no way she could tell
Simon about Edward. Not now, not yet, not while
both their marriage and friendship was so new and
fragile. She would just have to pray that she wasn't
found out. And since the only one who knew the
truth was Lord Killian, she would just have to make
sure he didn't recognize her when she saw him next.
With that in mind, Catherine went off to visit
Madeline's dressmaker almost eagerly.

"Are you choosing some clothes for yourself
also?" Catherine asked Madeline on the way to the
dressmaker's. "Or shall you be in mourning for a
while longer?"

Madeline had been watching the passing carriages
and turned to Catherine slowly. "I shall be wearing
black for about another six months, although I

shall mourn my brother's death for the rest of my life."

Some demon inside Catherine forced her to pursue the subject. "You must have been very fond of him."

"Fond is not exactly the word I'd use to describe my feelings for him," Madeline said. "I am fond of my brother Michael. He always had time for me as a child, and never minded my tagging along. Edward was more aloof. He was never a friend like Michael was, but someone to admire and respect. I was always so thrilled when he took a few minutes to speak to me."

What a charming picture Madeline painted! Catherine thought, though the other woman seemed unaware of how her words sounded and Catherine kept her face expressionless. "Why was he so different from Michael?"

"He was the heir." Madeline seemed surprised she had to ask.

"You mean he was looked upon as some sort of god just because he was your father's heir?"

"My father comes from a very old and important family," Madeline explained stiffly. "We are expected to be leaders in society, but the heir has an even more important responsibility. He must safeguard the Killian name for the future so that the memory of our ancestors is not tainted in any way. Both father and Edward believed in this very strongly."

"What an awful burden!"

Madeline looked away for a moment. "But it

wasn't just anyone. Edward was different. You would have had to know him to understand why we felt that way about him. He was the sort of man that inspired trust and respect. Everyone loved him. He was the very essence of gentlemanly honor."

Thankfully, the carriage pulled to a stop before the dressmaker's and Catherine used the few moments it took them to climb from the coach to compose her thoughts. How could the deceitful man that she had married be the paragon of virtue and honor that Madeline described?

The next few hours passed in almost painful slowness as Catherine stood for endless fittings as Madeline dictated styles and fabrics to the bustling team of seamstresses.

"Perhaps this skirt could be made a little fuller," Catherine suggested at one point as she stared at her reflection in a roughly stitched dress of deep blue voile. "It seems rather narrow."

"As you wish." Mrs. Cheering shrugged and wiped off the chalk markings she had made on the material.

Madeline swung around from where she had been choosing some ribbon trim and saw the seamstress removing the marks. "No one wears full skirts anymore!" she cried. "Leave it as it was."

Mrs. Cheering shrugged again and resumed the light sewing that she had been doing to hold the pieces of the skirt together.

"But it feels so constricting," Catherine complained. "I can barely walk in it."

Madeline's lips tightened. "Mrs. Cheering, do you

104

make any full skirts for ladies of fashion these days?"

The seamstress smiled apologetically at Catherine, then shook her head. "No, ma'am. Certainly not for anyone as slender as the young lady here."

Madeline gave Catherine a half smile, then turned back to the ribbons. She picked out several, then selected bolt after bolt of fabric for Catherine's approval for day dresses, evening wear.

"Oh, I do not know," Catherine hesitated as she saw even more material before her. A new dress or two was all she had planned for, all that she thought she needed to keep Lord Killian from recognizing her. To buy more seemed such a frivolous waste of Simon's money. "They all seem similar to the ones you already fit on me. Although that flowered material is pretty . . ." She trailed off with indecision.

"I do not see what the fuss is about." Madeline sighed with more patience. She turned to the seamstress, who was holding out samples of muslin for day dresses. "Make up a dress in each," she told the woman. "The same styles as the other, but make up the flowered and the lilac in long sleeves, the blue and green in short sleeves."

"But that will be four more dresses," Catherine protested. "We already ordered three."

Madeline just smiled and appeared to ignore her remark as she handed the seamstress some more ribbons, then waved the woman away. Once she was out of earshot, Madeline's tightly held smile was replaced by a look of annoyance.

"I do not appreciate being treated like an errant schoolgirl in front of the help," Madeline snarled. "It is quite obvious that you know nothing about what is in style in London these days. If you don't trust my judgment and want to look like some sort of quiz, then just say so. You need not humiliate me."

Catherine stared at Madeline in surprise. Her lightning-fast changes of mood were almost impossible to keep up with. "I didn't mean to hurt your feelings," she quickly assured her. "And I certainly wasn't questioning your judgment. I just didn't want to be extravagant and buy things that I did not need."

Madeline looked only partially forgiving. "But that is the problem," she pointed out. "You do not know what you need. This is London now, not the backwoods of Canada." Her eyes softened. "You don't want Simon to be ashamed of you, do you?"

"No, of course not."

Madeline smiled sweetly, and patted Catherine's hand. "Then just trust me," she said. Turning around, she called the seamstress back. "Show us some material for formal dresses now."

In a few moments one of the assistants staggered into the room, carrying bolts of satins, silks, and velvets. She laid them on the worktable, and one by one carried them over to Catherine to drape a length around her body so they could see how the color would look on her. Catherine liked the rose-colored velvet immediately, and a pale green satin, but Madeline seemed to favor the brighter colors.

"How many formal dresses will I need?" Catherine asked as the rose velvet was held up to her and she looked at her reflection in the full-length mirror before her.

"Oh, three or four should be enough to start with." Madeline pulled out a bright-red satin. "Try this."

Red had never been that becoming to her, and this material seemed especially garish, but Catherine said nothing. She'd become all too aware of the fact that she knew nothing about styles in London and she did not want to shame Simon or Mrs. Bradford. Though it seemed to go against her better judgment, she had to trust Madeline.

The seamstress carefully folded the length of rose velvet and replaced it on the table, then took the fabric that Madeline had indicated and draped it around Catherine.

"Why, that's perfect!" Madeline cried.

Catherine tried not to cringe. Surely there must be something else in style that would suit her better?

"You need something very special for Grandmother's dinner party, and this will be just the thing!" Perhaps Madeline saw the doubt in Catherine's eyes, for her smile widened. "Isn't that rose color lovely? And it's almost the exact fabric that Grandmother is going to wear that night."

"Oh, it is?" Catherine said with a sigh and a wistful glance that dismissed the rose velvet.

"But Grandmother does so love to see the young

107

people in bright colors," Madeline said, and began to issue orders to the seamstress as to what kind of dress to make.

As Catherine stood in front of the mirror, the seamstress and her two assistants began to drape the material, then cut it. With quick stitches they tacked the pieces together and sewed tiny tucks in just the right places until the dress began to take shape on Catherine's body. The material was soft and fell into gentle folds from an empire waist. A series of small tucks gave the bodice the fullness to cover her breasts and were repeated to give some puffiness to the small sleeves.

Madeline sat and watched as the women worked, occasionally making suggestions or ordering changes. "The neck must be cut lower," she decreed. The seamstress made the changes quickly with long running stitches. "Yes, that is much better."

Catherine looked down at herself aghast. Surely Madeline had not meant for it to be cut that low! Catherine knew that styles were different in London, but she would feel indecent in this dress! Madeline, however, was ignoring her pleading looks and frowning at the dress.

"The bodice is too full," Madeline announced. "It takes away from the sleeves."

The seamstress nodded her agreement, and hurriedly took a few tucks in the bodice. Catherine felt the material strain across her breasts. "Madeline . . ." she said hesitantly. "Are you certain—"

"For goodness' sakes, I do wish I had never come out with you! I promised Simon I would dress you

108

respectably, but you seem determined to disgrace us all." She ended with a pained sniff and looked ready to flounce out of the establishment in tears.

"Madeline, please," Catherine cried quickly. "It's just so different from what I have worn before. Will you be wearing a dress like it?"

"I am still in mourning," she reminded her. "My dress will have to be more subdued."

By the time the seamstress took the partially made dress off her, Catherine was despondent. The dress was far more revealing than any she had ever worn before, and she did not know how she would have the courage to wear it. She sighed and sat down in the nearest chair.

Madeline looked at her in surprise. "Are you tired? We need not do any more shopping today if you'd prefer not."

"If you do not mind," Catherine agreed quickly. "I do worry about leaving Teddy and—"

"We've ordered the most important things. The rest can wait."

Catherine smiled her thanks and went back into the dressing room to put her old dress back on. The shopping trip hadn't gone as she planned, and it was more her emotional worries that was tiring her out than worry over Teddy. She wished Anne had come with them; Catherine somehow knew she could trust Simon's sister. She wasn't nearly as certain of Madeline, though she had no real reason to feel that way.

As Catherine was dressing, Madeline followed Mrs. Cheering into the other room, pulling a five-pound note from her pocket as she did so. She slipped it into the seamstress's pocket as she spoke. "Why don't you make that neckline just a trifle lower?" she suggested softly.

The seamstress's hand unerringly found and closed around the money. "Whatever you say, Mrs. Marley."

By the time Catherine came back out, Madeline was waiting at the front door. "Wasn't this fun?" she asked Catherine brightly. "We'll have to do this again soon."

"Oh, he's such a darling little boy," Anne whispered as she peered over Catherine's shoulder at Teddy, sleeping peacefully in his crib. "Simon must be very proud of him, although it is difficult to imagine him as a father."

Catherine smiled weakly and tucked Teddy's blanket a little closer around him, then bent to kiss his forehead. It was the same day as her shopping expedition with Madeline, but dinner was over and the men were having their port while Catherine and Anne had come to check on the baby. Catherine still wasn't used to leaving Teddy with someone else. "Come get me if you have any problem with him during the night," she told the plump middle-aged woman who was knitting by the fire.

"Oh, he'll be right fine now, don't you worry none."

"Bessie knows all there is about babies," Anne assured her, taking Catherine's arm and leading her out of the nursery. "We were lucky to get her."

"I'm sure she is quite competent, still—"

Anne pulled Catherine down the hall. "I know, it's the first time you have left him with someone else, so it is only normal to be concerned. But you must remember that you have a whole family here now that wants their turn to fuss and spoil him shamelessly. I know I intend to be a doting old maid."

Anne's words awoke the dozing guilt in her heart. "You mustn't say things like that," Catherine chided her softly as they walked down the hall. "You are still young. There's no reason why you won't have your own family one day. I doubt that your fiancé would have wanted you to remain alone the rest of your life."

Anne put her other hand over Catherine's and squeezed it with a slight smile. "Oh, please," she sighed. "Don't start with that argument also. Grandmother and Simon have both told me the same thing, but they just don't understand that if I cannot marry the man that I love, I would rather be alone. Wouldn't you feel that way?"

Anne's question startled Catherine. Not because it showed the strength of Anne's love for Edward, but because Catherine had never thought about it in terms of herself. Could she have been willing to marry Simon if she had truly loved Edward? Shouldn't she have felt repulsed by the very idea of sharing her life with someone other than Edward, even if her circumstances had left her little real choice? Did that mean that she hadn't loved him?

Anne took Catherine's arm. "That is really why I am so glad that Simon married you instead of Madeline," Anne whispered confidentially. "He really must be over that silly infatuation he had with her when they were young."

"You think so?" Catherine murmured. "She certainly is attractive."

"Yes, but he married you, not her."

Except that was not proof of anything, as Catherine knew only too well.

They went back to the drawing room in silence and found Madeline was sitting on a chair near a window, paging restlessly through a book that she put down when Anne and Catherine came in. "It is about time you two came back," she complained. "I think it was rude of you to go off and leave me."

Catherine blushed at the reprimand although she and Anne had made no secret of their destination when they left the dinner table. Madeline could have joined them had she wished.

"Where's Grandmother?" Anne asked.

"She's looking for some yarn," Madeline said. "She wants to make a cap or something for the baby."

"Oh, yes. I believe she mentioned it at dinner," Catherine said as the door swung open and Mrs. Bradford came in, followed by Nigel and Simon, who had just finished their after-dinner port.

Madeline's face lost its pout with the arrival of the others, but some of her gloom appeared to return after Mrs. Bradford joined Anne, Simon joined Catherine, and Nigel went to get himself a

brandy. Madeline got to her feet, shook the wrinkles from her skirt, and walked gracefully to where
the others were sitting.

"It must be very hard to adjust to so different a
way of life from what you were used to in Canada,"
she said to Catherine with sweet sympathy. "I imagine that you are just terrified about taking your
place in society."

"Not really," Catherine said. There were other,
more pressing worries.

"Why should she be?" Simon sounded slightly
annoyed.

Madeline just continued to smile sweetly. "But
just think of all the things you'll have to become
accustomed to," she murmured. "Everyone's
title . . ."

"That's no harder than keeping track of everyone's name," Simon pointed out.

Madeline's shrug was graceful. "Social etiquette is
much more rigid here. One little mistake could
mean a ruined reputation."

Catherine was only too aware of that. And knew
it didn't have to be a real mistake even, but an
imagined one. Or one you were accused of, as Lord
Killian had accused her of not really being married
to Edward.

Mrs. Bradford wasn't sharing Madeline's worries
though and looked up from her knitting. "Oh,
pooh," she scoffed. "All it takes is a little common
sense to stay out of trouble, and Catherine has
plenty of that. There's no need to get her all worried for nothing."

"I wasn't trying to worry her," Madeline protested. "I was merely trying to help."

"Ah, yes. How cruel of everyone to question your motives," Nigel said. "Well, you must let it be on their heads if she eats with her fingers or trips while she is waltzing. Then everyone will be sorry they did not listen to you!" Nigel went past them and sat in a large chair in the corner. He sipped his brandy slowly, seemingly already having forgotten everyone else's presence.

Catherine dragged her eyes away from him and turned to Simon. "Do you waltz here?"

"Of course," Madeline answered for him. "Didn't you in Canada?"

"I have seen it done, but since I was in mourning for my father, I never had the chance to learn it for myself."

"How very awkward!" Madeline cried.

"Not at all," Simon said, quickly getting to his feet. "It is a simple dance. We can teach it to her now." He held out his hand and Catherine put hers into it. His touch was warm and safe. She let her hold on him tighten slightly. He responded with a smile as Madeline jumped to her feet.

"Wouldn't it be better to let her watch it being done first?" she asked. "I would be happy to partner you and we could show . . ."

Catherine was willing to acquiesce, but Simon tightened his hold on her. "It is not that difficult a dance. Anne, would you play a waltz for us on the pianoforte?" he asked, then turned his gentle smile toward Catherine as he led her to a clear space in the middle of the room. "Relax."

"I feel as if I am on show."

"No one will be critical." And his smile was so disarmingly understanding that she almost believed him.

Anne began to play a simple waltz melody while Simon led Catherine through the steps of the dance. She followed him easily, for there was a splendor flowing with the gentle call of the music. Or was it being in his arms that made her heart feel like singing while her feet seemed to fly? His hand on her back was magic, lighting a fire in her soul, its warmth spreading out to her fingers and toes and stealing her breath at the same time.

"You're a fast learner," Simon said quietly. "You must have been a good dancer back home."

"Oh, no." She was quick to disclaim all credit. "It is because you are so good at leading."

Simon's hold on her tightened. Or was it just his hold on her heart? "Perhaps we are well matched," he said under his breath.

"Perhaps." But she liked that idea and held it closely to her as they moved to the music, his hand guiding her as their breaths, their hearts, beat in unison. Might she dare to hope that what began as a desperate grab for safety on her part was turning into something real? Her flickering smile of hope faltered slightly when the music stopped. She let go of Simon, but he kept his arm around her shoulders. The little smile flickered again in her heart.

"That was done quite nicely," Mrs. Bradford said. "It was a pleasure to watch you."

"Shall I play another tune?" Anne asked.

Madeline stood up. "Only if I may take a turn around the floor with Simon."

"I am sure Nigel would be happy to oblige," Simon said.

Madeline flounced back into a chair and, when Anne began another piece, Simon took up Catherine's hands again. She could dance with him forever, Catherine thought, losing herself in the sway of the music and the feel of his body so near hers. She could rest in his arms for eternity, she realized, then frowned as she thought she felt a change in Simon's movements.

"Is your leg bothering you?" she asked.

He shrugged away her question for a moment, leading her through a turn. But as they twirled in the confines of the small space, she could feel a twinge of pain shoot through him, and he lost step, causing Catherine to stumble against him. She dropped his hand and stood still.

"It's not quite as easy as it looks, is it?" Madeline said.

Simon ignored Madeline's words as he brought Catherine's hand to his lips. "I'm sorry, my dear. I might have been strong enough to return to battle, but obviously I am not yet up to the rigors of a London season." His lips brushed her hand, leaving a fire burning on her skin and in her soul.

"I was tiring myself," she said.

Her voice sounded breathless and weak, but no one seemed to notice but her as Simon limped over to the sofa. Nigel offered him a brandy, and the talk progressed from the guest list of the party to the condition of the estate. No more was said about dancing, though Catherine could still feel the touch of Simon's hand on her back and feel the strength of his guidance through the dance steps. No, not just Simon's hand. Her husband's hand.

Chapter Seven

Catherine looked at her reflection in the tall mirror in her room and frowned. The red satin dress that Madeline had ordered for her was as hideous as Catherine had feared it would be. What's more, it did not fit very comfortably—the waist and the sleeves were far too tight and the neckline was cut outrageously low.

Catherine tugged at the bodice, trying somehow to make the tiny strip of material cover the wide expanse of her chest that was still exposed, but she gave up with an exasperated sigh. London fashions were certainly different from the current styles in Halifax.

Her first idea had been to cover up the front of the dress somehow, and a quick search of her wardrobe turned up two shawls—one a pale yellow and the other black. They both were too shabby to consider wearing.

This was ridiculous, she thought. She was behaving like a silly schoolgirl just because the neckline of this dress was a little lower than her other dresses. She had a responsibility to Simon and his family to look her best. She had better become accustomed to London fashions, no matter how outrageous they seemed. One thing was certain, this dress was about as different as any dress could be from the one Lord Killian had seen her in. He certainly would not be able to connect that shabbily dressed waif with Simon's wife.

With that comforting thought, Catherine walked back to the mirror to take a final look at herself before she went down to meet the guests, but as soon as she saw the way the shiny red fabric clung to her body, all her bravado disappeared. She wrapped her arms across her chest and sat down in a nearby chair in despair. What was she to do?

The door to Simon's dressing room opened and with a sigh Catherine rose slowly to her feet, turning to face him with reluctance. He looked quite elegant in a black coat and breeches. His white shirt looked crisp and neat beneath a waistcoat of white and silver brocade. Although he still walked with a trace of a limp, Catherine barely noticed it. She was aware only of how well his fashionable dress seemed to suit him, of how his presence always seemed to make her heart race and her breath disappear.

His air of assurance made her feel even more ill at ease. How could she take her place beside him downstairs and meet his friends if she was so embarrassed about her appearance? She could not keep her arms crossed over her chest all evening, nor could she peek out at the guests from behind draperies.

"It's no use," she cried out suddenly, flinging her arms wide and looking down at her dress. "I just cannot do it!"

Sensing that Simon was staring at her, she folded her arms across her chest once more and lifted her tear-filled eyes up to his startled ones.

"I am sorry if it will embarrass you or your grandmother, but I cannot wear this dress! I have tried to make myself go downstairs in it, but I just can't." She turned away from him and added more quietly, "I feel like a strumpet!"

"Which is remarkably similar to how you look!"

Catherine turned around to stare at him. She had never seen such anger in his eyes.

"Whatever possessed you to order such a ghastly dress? You couldn't honestly believe that such vulgarity was acceptable, could you?"

"But I did not—"

"Let's just hope that you have something else that is presentable," Simon snapped, hurrying over to her wardrobe. He quickly searched through the dresses hanging there. Only a few of her new things had arrived, and they, along with most of the dresses she brought with her from Canada, were for day wear. That left her blue silk and her wedding dress.

Simon pulled out the white satin and frowned as he turned it around in his hand. "This is a bit too formal," he said. "But it is far better than that hideous thing you have on." He tossed the dress onto the bed as he walked across to the door. "Shall I ring for your maid to come back, or can you manage by yourself?"

"I can manage alone." She waited in the center of the room until he left.

Simon's immediate assumption that she had chosen the awful dress had infuriated her, as did his refusal to listen to her explanation, but she quickly realized that she had an even greater problem — Madeline. Where Catherine could claim inexperience as an excuse for buying such an awful dress, Madeline could not. She was fully aware of what was in fashion and what was considered acceptable for someone in Catherine's position, yet she had deliberately chosen something offensive.

Catherine shivered slightly as she reached behind her to unfasten her dress. Why would Madeline hate her so? Madeline had already given Simon up when she married Nigel.

Simon took a deep calming breath before he joined his family in the drawing room, trying not to think of the scandal that might have occurred had Catherine actually appeared in that dress. It could have taken years to undo the damage to her reputation.

A footman on his way down the stairs gave Simon a curious glance as he passed by, for Simon appeared to be staring at a watercolor painting of a vase. Simon shook himself slightly and started down the stairs, suddenly aware that his wife was a virtual stranger to him. They had conversed briefly on board the ship and had traveled to London together, but Simon really knew nothing about her. She was a convenient way out of an idiotic dilemma he had put himself into. She had seemed unexceptional, pleasant in personality and appearance, so he had married her, never considering that she might be totally unsuitable for the role.

"Ah, Simon, there you are." His grandmother joined him at the bottom of the stairs. "Where's Catherine? Isn't she ready yet? The guests will be arriving any moment."

Simon stopped to readjust his cravat in a mirror and put the last of his shock back under covers. "She should be right down," he said. "She was just making some last minute changes."

Mrs. Bradford sighed. "I do hope she isn't too nervous. There is no reason for her to be. She is such a lovely girl and obviously well bred. We love her and so will everyone else."

His grandmother's words took a few moments to wash away the last of his worries, but they did. She was right, he realized as he watched her go into the drawing room. There never had been any hint of anything improper in Catherine's actions, or her dress up to now. The clothing she had brought with her from Halifax was not all the best quality, but none was garish or indecent. So why would she suddenly chose something so vulgar?

Simon followed his grandmother into the drawing room, frowning over this latest puzzle. Perhaps it was just her inexperience or maybe she had never had the funds to order whatever she wanted and the brightness of the material had attracted her. He stopped just inside the door, realizing he had not been very kind to Catherine about the dress. Instead of explaining to her why the dress was so offensive and suggesting that it might be best to change to something else, he had stormed about, officiously issuing orders.

Feeling rather guilty, Simon turned around to go back upstairs. The least he could do was see if she was ready to come down and accompany her. His grandmother was right. She was probably feeling very nervous and his condemnation of her dress would certainly not have helped her relax.

"Oh, Simon," Madeline called, gliding up beside him from across the room. "Where is Catherine? Is she going to make a grand entrance once the guests are here?" Taking his arm, she added, "Do come sit with me. We have had so little time to visit since you have come home."

Gently removing his arm from her grasp, he edged slightly away. There was something about Madeline, something false and studied, as if she were playing a part. How had he ever thought he loved her? "Catherine was not quite ready, but I was going back up to hurry her along," he said. "I doubt that a grand entrance is much in her style." He shuddered involuntarily at the thought of

Catherine and that dress.

"Oh, dear, you've seen the dress," Madeline whispered, a look of pain crossing her face as she put her hand lightly on Simon's arm to detain him. "I had so hoped that she would not wear it."

Simon stopped, suspicion filling his heart. "What do you know of her dress?"

Madeline smiled sadly and shook her head. "I went with her to order her clothes. It was the least I could do for your bride, but I'm afraid that my help was not appreciated."

"Oh?"

"She insisted on ordering that horrid dress in spite of my assurances that it was improper. I told her it was most vulgar, and you would never approve of it, but she just laughed." When Simon said nothing, Madeline went on. "I don't imagine that she told it quite the same way though. No doubt it was all my fault, according to her. I am certain that she lost no time blaming me."

Doubts and suspicions had become certainties. "Actually, your name was not mentioned," Simon said coldly. "But I have no doubts now that it should have been. Your sly insults of the last few days have not gone unnoticed. Were you always this bitter, and I too blind to notice, or did something happen while I was away to sour you so?" He did not wait for an answer, but removed her hand from his arm and turned away.

* * *

124

Catherine changed her dress as quickly as possible, relieved not to be wearing that awful creation, but still shaken from Simon's anger. Not that he hadn't had every right to be angry, but knowing that wasn't the same as having her hands stop their shaking. What if she made some other mistake this evening? What if Lord Killian came and recognized her?

She longed, more than anything, for a friend she could talk to, someone to confide in. And though everyone had been quite kind, there was no one she could tell the truth to. The only person that she felt she could depend on was Mrs. Bradford, and even that could change if that lady learned that Simon was not Teddy's father. Simon was too unpredictable, Anne was still grieving for Edward, and Madeline was just plain dangerous. Catherine's apprehension grew as she went down the stairs to the drawing room.

"Why, how lovely you look," Mrs. Bradford exclaimed as Catherine came slowly into the room.

Luckily the guests had not begun to arrive yet, so Catherine had a few minutes more to compose herself. Mrs. Bradford hurried over and took Catherine's hands, holding them out from her sides to admire her dress.

"Don't tell me that you ordered this dress here in London," the older woman said. "There couldn't have been time for all this fine detail."

"No, actually, the other dress just wasn't right," Catherine said awkwardly, carefully avoiding Simon's glance. Instead, she caught the tail end of an angry glare that Madeline sent her way before turning to inspect the flowers on the table. "I hope this one will be acceptable."

Nigel sauntered over to them. "I find it quite charming," he told Catherine quietly. "It makes you look very young and unworldly. Quite a change for London society."

His courtesy, always surprising and seeming so out of character, eased her frayed nerves. "Actually this was my wedding dress," she admitted.

"It's beautiful," Mrs. Bradford said, squeezing her hand. "I'm so happy that I have the chance to see it on you. I can almost imagine what the wedding itself was like."

Simon coughed uneasily from close behind Catherine, startling her slightly. "I think I hear someone arriving," he said.

There was no chance for them to speak privately, but his eyes told her he was no longer angry and almost seemed to be asking her forgiveness. She smiled at him, somewhat uncertainly at first, for fear she might be misreading his gaze, wanting to see things in it that he didn't intend. But then he took her hand and squeezed it gently as they went to meet their guests.

The next hour passed quickly for Catherine. The guests were mostly old family friends who welcomed her warmly, and teased Simon gently about his surprising status of husband and father. By the time most of the guests had arrived, Catherine was

126

feeling very much at ease. How silly she had been to think that she had no friends. Everyone was being so wonderful to her. She turned toward Simon to ask him about someone she had just met, when suddenly her heart leapt up into her throat, and she felt herself go pale. There, in the doorway, was Edward.

As Catherine stared aghast, the man moved closer to them. She felt incapable of movement or speech, and although she knew Simon was speaking, she did not hear the words.

"Why, Michael, it's about time you arrived," Simon laughed as they shook hands. "I feared you had gone back to the country."

"Not without meeting your wife." The man smiled, and as he spoke, Catherine breathed a sigh of relief. This was not Edward, but someone who looked startlingly like him.

Simon took Catherine's hand. "Catherine, this is Madeline's brother, Michael Corbett-Smith," Simon said, apparently not noticing her sudden start. "And Michael, this is Catherine, my wife."

"I am delighted to meet you." Michael smiled. He took her other hand, and kissed it gently. "Anyone who has managed to get Simon to the altar must be quite a prize." Catherine smiled uneasily, and managed to pull her hand out of his as he turned back to Simon.

"I must tell you how pleased I am, old boy," Michael went on. "Always said that you were too good for my sister."

Catherine opened her mouth to speak only to find that shock had robbed her of her voice. She cleared her throat and tried again. "Is your father here?" she managed to whisper hoarsely.

Michael turned to look at her. "No, I'm afraid he could not make it, but I am certain that he will be sorry that he did not attend."

Catherine's eyes closed briefly in relief as Michael and Simon laughed over some remark. So her new identity would not be tested just yet. Maybe it never would be, if she could just find the right moment to tell Simon the truth.

Dinner was announced a few minutes later, and Catherine found herself seated between an old colonel who was a distant cousin of Mrs. Bradford's, and a Mr. Lockwood, a man of about Simon's age whose protruding belly proclaimed that his main interest in dinner was the food, not his table partners.

She should have enjoyed the occasional conversation between the removes of the delicious meal, but for the misfortune of sitting across the table from Michael. He did nothing that was in any way threatening to her, but his very presence was a constant reminder of potential trouble. Too nervous to eat, Catherine merely picked at her food, sending back most of her delicately cooked fish and succulent pheasant untouched. It was with great relief that she left the men to their port.

Much to Catherine's astonishment, she was not the only one who was not glad to have Michael present. "Why did they have to invite Madeline's brother?" Anne grumbled as she sat down next to Catherine in the drawing room.

Catherine looked at her in surprise. She agreed with Anne's sentiments, but could hardly say so. "He seems nice," she said lamely.

"Nice!" Anne scoffed. "He is heartless. An insensitive boor." Leaning back, she folded her arms crossly and glared ahead of her.

Catherine gazed around the room, sending a warm smile to all who had turned at the sound of Anne's outburst. "Whatever did he do?" Catherine whispered a moment later.

Anne turned her head, and saw Catherine's puzzled look. She sighed, and let her hands fall to her lap. "Oh, you must think I am a fool," she said slowly. "But I do wish that he would go back to his estate in the country, and I would not have to see him. You know I was engaged to his brother?" she asked. Catherine nodded silently. "Well, Michael's presence here only serves to remind me of all that had happened. Every time I see him, all the old hurts come back."

"You mean because he looks so like him?" Catherine whispered sympathetically, not aware until the words were spoken that she should have had no way of knowing that.

"Yes, that is part of it," Anne nodded. Thankfully, she had forgotten that Catherine supposedly had never met Edward. "If they weren't so alike, perhaps I could forget," she murmured.

Catherine squeezed her hand, wishing that she

could tell her somehow that Edward had not been worth all the devotion lavished on him, but if Anne had loved him so, and was cherishing his memory, what purpose would there be in telling her the truth? It would only cause Anne more pain, and probably ruin the friendship that was starting to grow between them.

Once the men had finished their port, they came into the drawing room also. Simon started to come toward Catherine and Anne, but was waylaid by a stout dowager who wanted to hear about his experiences in the war. He smiled apologetically at his wife, and followed the older lady across the room.

Catherine watched as Simon settled himself amid some of his friends, then she turned back to Anne with a quiet sigh, only to discover they were no longer alone. Michael had joined them, and Anne was staring stonily ahead of her.

"How good of you to join us, Mr. Corbett-Smith," Catherine murmured politely with a furtive glance at Anne.

"You must call me Michael," he insisted quickly. His smile was warm and friendly, and Catherine felt herself softening slightly. "Simon and I have always been good friends, so I am certain that we shall be seeing a lot of each other.

"The families must be very close," Catherine said with a weak smile.

"We practically live in one another's pockets in the country," Anne noted cynically.

"Oh." Catherine looked from Anne's forbidding

130

face to Michael's openly friendly one. "Is your estate close to Mrs. Bradford's?" she asked.

"It is my father's estate," Michael corrected her. "But . . ."

"But it will be yours someday, will it not?" Anne asked bitterly. "You have run it all these years, and probably wished it would be yours, so you ought to be happy that Edward conveniently stepped out of the way for you." Anne jumped to her feet and darted through the guests toward the door.

Catherine watched her leave in horror, and turned quickly back to Michael. He was staring down at his hands.

"I am certain that she did not mean that," Catherine said quietly. "She has been upset for some reason tonight."

Michael looked up at her, his eyes filled with sadness. "She is upset because I came," he said bitterly. "You see, no one can quite forgive me for not being my brother."

Catherine reached out and gently put her hand on his arm. "You know that is not true. Anne would not be that mean. She is not the sort to blame you for being alive while her fiancé is dead."

"No?" He shrugged. "She might not, but I fear my father does. You see, I was the one that wanted to join the army, but no, Father decided that I had to stay at home and run the estate. He bought a commission for Edward and proudly paraded him about in his uniform. You can imagine how he felt when we heard that Edward had been killed—he wished that he had let me go as I had wanted and kept Edward safely in London with him."

"Oh, Michael, did he actually tell you that?" Catherine cried softly. "Maybe he just said it when he was extremely upset and not really himself."

Michael smiled cynically. "Since that time he has continually tried to make me into my brother. I have to take up his interests and his friends. I am surprised that he has not suggested that I change my name to Edward."

"You must not let him do it," Catherine said firmly. "I think I would much rather have the real you for a friend than a copy of your brother. I am afraid that what I have heard of him has made him sound too high in the instep for me."

Michael nodded. "He was not a bad sort, really, but all that attention ruined his common sense. But do not let anyone hear me say that, or I would be drawn and quartered." He laughed with a quick glance around them and looked up as Simon approached them.

"You know, Michael, if I did not trust Catherine so, I would think you are trying to steal her away from me." Simon laughed, and sat down on the other side of his wife.

Michael smiled. "Believe me, if I thought I could, I would." He reached over, picked up Catherine's hand, and brought it gently to his lips as he stood up. "I am not certain what you did to deserve such a treasure for your wife, but I do envy you."

Simon smiled at Catherine's blushing face, and

took her other hand. "Perhaps you should look more diligently for someone of your own," Simon teased.

Michael nodded, but Catherine saw the look of pain cross his face first. "I shall have to do that." He bowed to Catherine. "Thank you for being such an understanding listener," he said, then he turned to join another group of the guests.

Although the evening was much more pleasant than Catherine had expected, she was not unhappy when she was able to retire to her room. The guests had been quite friendly, but after Simon's anger over the dress and the shock of meeting Edward's brother, Catherine had never been able to relax enough to truly enjoy herself. Even after the guests had left, she was still tense because she knew that she had to have a talk with Simon. She could not delay any longer telling him that she had been married to Edward.

After her maid had unpinned Catherine's hair and brushed all the tangles out, she helped her out of her dress and into a pale blue nightgown. Catherine put on a matching dressing gown and sat on her window seat, gazing out at the night sky while the maid tidied up the room. When Catherine's dress had been hung back into the wardrobe and her dressing table cleared of clutter, the maid bid her good night, and slipped from the room. Catherine continued to stare out the window, mulling over the problem of her first marriage. She hadn't set out to deceive Simon, but suddenly that's all it seemed.

A quiet knock sounded on the door to the dressing room, and Catherine turned toward it in surprise. She rose to her feet slowly as the door opened and Simon came in.

"I hope I am not disturbing you," he said.

"No, of course not," Catherine said. She took a few steps away from the window as he came in and closed the door.

"I wanted to apologize to you for the way I acted about your dress earlier this evening," he told her. "I am afraid that I was rather hasty in my condemnation of your taste and judgment. I did not even give you the chance to explain how you happened to have gotten that monstrosity."

Simon looked so contrite that Catherine had to smile. "It is kind of you to apologize, but I did understand your anger."

"My anger perhaps, but there was no reason for my rudeness." Simon seemed determined to point out the full extent of his guilt to her.

Catherine smiled a little more. "I should think the dress would have been reason enough," she laughed. "I was much more comfortable in my old dress, even if it was out of style."

Simon moved toward the center of the room. "You looked truly lovely in it," he said gently. His eyes seemed softer as they gazed at her, softer and flickering with warmth. "I hope that it did not

134

bring back painful memories by wearing it."

This seemed to be the perfect chance to tell Simon about Edward, but Catherine was afraid to begin. That warmth in his eyes was being answered by a flame in her soul, a burning, a yearning to be held. Simon took a step closer to her, taking her hand into his.

"Everyone seemed most impressed by you," he went on. "I cannot tell you the number of compliments I received on my choice of a bride."

Catherine smiled weakly with a blush. Near him her thoughts seemed jumbled and incoherent. "I am glad that I did not disappoint you or your grandmother," she said. "Everyone has been so kind to me, I would hate to feel that I let you down."

Simon's mouth bent into a frown. "You make it sound as if you were a charity case. You have every right to demand that we not let you down also. You are a member of the family, you know."

"Oh, I know." Catherine shrugged. Simon let go of her hand and she walked over to sit on the edge of the bed, trying to escape that power he seemed to have over her will. "I cannot help but remember why we married."

"And why did we?" Simon prompted her, coming over to sit next to her.

His leg brushed hers just slightly, but it seemed to singe her heart. "Because I was in a rather desperate situation," Catherine said grimly.

"To which marriage was not the only solution," Simon noted. "It might have been possible to legally force your husband's family to provide for you."

Catherine ignored his last remark and brushed imaginary lint from her dressing gown. "I just feel like a fraud when everyone fusses over me. We married only because it was convenient for both of us, and sometimes it is hard to pretend that we have been married for more than a year."

"We do not really get along that badly," Simon pointed out. His voice had changed, grown hoarser.

"Oh, no," Catherine quickly said. "I never meant we did."

"In fact," Simon said as he picked up her hand again. "I think we get along remarkably well. Perhaps I was only using Madeline and Nigel as an excuse to marry you."

The heat in Catherine's heart spread to her cheeks as Simon leaned forward slowly and kissed her gently on her lips. He pulled back with a smile. "I have been wanting to do that for some time now," he admitted.

Catherine just stared back at him. "Have you?" she whispered. As long as she'd been wanting him to?

Simon leaned forward again, and this time, as his lips touched hers, his arms went around her to draw her closer to him. His kiss was gentle at first, but as he felt her response to him, it became more demanding, a fire wanting to grow and consume all in its path.

After a time, his lips left hers, but Simon's arms continued to hold her close. His lips tickled her ear before moving down her neck and wreaking havoc with her heartbeat.

Oh, how she loved the feel of his arms around her, the warm protection of his embrace. She moved even closer to him, until she could feel the thick velvet of his dressing gown pressing against her breasts and knew a deeper longing for his touch. She lifted her arms to encircle his neck, and turned her head to meet his lips as they came back to hers.

Their kiss seemed to last forever, until Catherine felt all her breath had been drawn from her body. But when Simon finally lifted his lips from hers, she sensed that he had withdrawn from her in spirit too. Instinctively, she realized that he was letting her decide whether or not he stay and make love to her. If she was not ready to have him as a lover, then he would go back to his dressing room to sleep.

Catherine, however, did not want him to go. She knew as her head lay against his chest that she very much wanted him to stay. A small part of that wish was the realization that as she became more important to him, Madeline would mean less and less, but it was more than that. She was Simon's wife now, and she wanted to belong to him completely. She wanted to feel that she was really and truly his wife and a part of his life.

Gently, she took one hand from around his neck and slid it inside his dressing gown, running it through the dark hairs on his chest. She felt beneath her fingertips the hard muscles of his body, letting her fingers come to rest at the base of his neck.

Simon suddenly took her hand in his and raised it to his lips. She turned her face to look up at him, letting him read her acceptance of him in her eyes.

With a sigh Simon let go of her hand and bent to kiss her again. His kiss was rougher this time, his tongue parting her lips to explore her mouth as he let his weight against her push her back onto the cover of the bed.

As Simon's hands caressed her body, the thought of Edward nagged briefly at her. Tomorrow, she thought, as she gave herself up to Simon's lovemaking. She would tell him tomorrow.

Chapter Eight

Nigel frowned at his wife, unmoved by the lovely picture she presented as she sat in her bed sipping hot chocolate. Her long dark hair fell in soft curls onto her shoulders, and the deep blue of her bed jacket accented her creamy white skin.

"I do not wish to hear any of the details," he said curtly, cutting her off as she was about to speak. "I know enough from what I heard last night to be certain that you were involved, and I was disgusted."

Madeline glared at him. "Why does everyone assume that I was at fault? Did no one ever think that perhaps Simon's milksop wife has no taste?"

"That could be quite possible," Nigel agreed coldly. "But you had accompanied her to prevent the very sort of thing that happened, so whichever of you ordered the dress, my dear, were at fault."

A quiet knock sounded on the door, and Madeline's maid peered into the room. "Would ya be wantin' to get up now?" she asked Madeline.

"Yes," Madeline agreed, pushing the tray on her lap to one side. "I am certain Mr. Marley will excuse us."

Nigel was not quite so amenable, however. "I am afraid that I shall not excuse you," he snapped, then turned to glare fiercely at the young girl who had stopped just inside the door. "Mrs. Marley will ring for you when she is ready."

The girl curtsied awkwardly, and fled out the door.

"Really, Nigel." Madeline's voice was angry. "I do not appreciate being contradicted in front of the servants."

"Then do not dismiss me as if I were one of them," he retorted.

Madeline sighed loudly, and threw back the cover on her bed. She stood up and slipped her feet into the soft velvet slippers that lay next to the bed. "I do not understand what all this fuss is about," she cried, changing from anger to sorely tried patience. "I was doing it only for us."

Nigel's eyebrows rose in disbelief as she went on. "I was only trying to protect what is ours." She moved closer to him, and let one hand run gently along the neckline of his green superfine coat.

Unmoved by such tactics, he took her hand down. "Which is?"

"Which is Bradleigh, of course," Madeline cried. She took a step away, and spun around to look at him. "You have worked that estate for all these years, and I will not see you thrown out now that Simon's returned."

"Your loyalty does you great credit," he said cynically, noting Madeline's sudden blush. "But I find it hard to understand your deep attachment to Bradleigh. You have repeatedly refused invitations to accompany me there because of more interesting engagements in the city."

"That does not mean that I want you to lose everything to Simon," Madeline pointed out.

"I would hardly be losing everything if he takes over Bradleigh," Nigel noted. "Grandmother has been very generous with the profits I have made from the estate. By various investments I have managed to accumulate a tidy fortune. I could easily buy us another estate near Bradleigh, or a house of our own here in town."

"It would not be the same as Bradleigh," Madeline insisted.

Nigel gave her a long look, then turned and walked to the door. With his hand on the knob, he faced her once more. "I want all these tricks stopped," he warned her. "Your attempts to discredit Catherine succeed only in making you look petty and mean, and reflect badly on our whole family."

Madeline turned away, her face set in mutinous determination.

"I mean it," Nigel repeated. "Another escapade like last night, and we shall take a long visit to my estate in Kent. A very long visit," he added.

When Madeline continued to stand with her back to him, Nigel opened the door and left. As soon as the door closed behind him though, she swung around to glare at it furiously.

"You cannot force me to stop," she whispered angrily after him. "I shall get that estate for Father, no matter how you threaten me." Although, she thought suddenly, there might be ways of doing it so that Nigel need never know she was involved. She walked thoughtfully over to the bell pull and rang for her maid.

"Oh, do buy that pair also," Anne urged. She and Catherine were in Pantheon's Bazaar, looking through an assortment of kid gloves. Catherine had found one soft white pair that she liked, but just as she was about to pay for them, she spotted a pink pair with tiny daisies embroidered around the wrist. Catherine tried to make a choice between the two pairs, but Anne thought she should just buy them both.

"You must have a dress that each pair would go with," Anne said. "And if not, why that is a marvelous excuse to go out and buy another dress."

"Oh, no," Catherine said, shaking her head. "I have more than enough dresses, especially with the three formal ones you helped me choose today." She put back the pink pair of gloves as a salesclerk came over to help them.

"My, my." Anne laughed. "Simon must have you

on a very tight budget." She picked up the pink gloves and handed them to the clerk along with Catherine's white pair. "We will take both pairs," Anne said quickly before Catherine could contradict her.

The clerk nodded and quickly wrapped the two pairs up in tissue paper, then in heavier brown paper. Catherine paid with a one-pound note, dropping the coins she received in change into her reticule as they walked out into the afternoon sunshine.

"Where would you like to go now?" Anne asked. "We could go to the lending library, or perhaps for a walk in the park."

Catherine looked around her uncertainly. "Perhaps we ought to go back home," she worried. "Simon may have returned and be wondering where I am."

"Oh, pooh!" Anne scoffed as she took Catherine's arm and began to stroll down the street with her. "He is gone to see his lawyers on business and will be there for hours, I am sure. And even if he did return before us, Grandmother will tell him where we have gone. Oh, my," Anne cried suddenly, pulling Catherine to a stop in front of a millinery shop. "Look at that hat." She giggled.

The store window held only one hat, but it was of monstrous proportions. The crown of the hat was covered in deep green velvet, but could barely be seen under a large bouquet of red velvet roses that was sewn into it. In among the roses a long strip of some frothy green material was woven, ending in the back in a huge bow. From the center of the bow three red ostrich plumes rose magnificently above the hat, their tips bending down slightly to sway in graceful rhythm when the hat was worn.

"Do woman actually wear such creations here in London?" Catherine murmured as she gazed at the hat in something akin to horror.

Anne shook her head, trying to suppress another giggle. "Not often," she assured Catherine. "And I have never seen one this ridiculous before."

"I do not think I could hold my head up if I had it on." Catherine laughed.

"On me, it would tend to brush the ceilings." Anne smiled.

"You ladies certainly seem to be enjoying yourselves," a voice said from behind them.

Anne and Catherine spun around to see Michael Corbett-Smith before them. After an uneasy glance at Anne, Catherine turned to him with a friendly smile.

"How nice to see you again," she said. "We were just trying to decide which one of us should buy that lovely hat." She nodded toward the window.

Michael groaned as he saw the hat, took both of them by the arm, and led them away. "For the sake of my friendship with Simon, I had better keep you away from there," he said with a laugh. He stopped a few doors down, when they stood before a stationer's shop. "This looks harmless enough."

"But not nearly as much fun." Catherine pouted

playfully. She glanced at Anne, expecting some sort of outburst from her, but she was standing stiffly on the other side of Michael, watching the carriages passing them by.

Michael seemed unaware of Anne's lack of attention. "Where are you ladies heading to?" he asked. "Might I have the pleasure of accompanying you?"

Anne did look over at him then. "We do not want to put you to any inconvenience," she said stiffly.

Considering Anne's rude treatment of him the previous night at the party, Catherine would not have been surprised if he left them without a word. Instead, he laughed, his friendly demeanor firmly in place. "My paltry plans are completely forgotten when placed beside the chance to escort two such lovely ladies somewhere," he said smoothly.

Catherine blushed slightly, embarrassed for Anne, for Michael's fine manners made Anne's curtness seem very mean. But Michael had not meant his words as a reprimand, and his eyes were gentle as he looked down at Anne.

"Now, where may I take you?" he repeated.

Catherine expected Anne to decide they were going home, but to her surprise, Anne merely shrugged her shoulders in confusion and looked back up at Michael. "We had finished our shopping and had not decided what to do next," she admitted.

"Capital!" Michael cried. "Then you two are all mine for the next few hours."

"The next few hours," Catherine cried in surprise. "Ought we to be out that long?"

"Just what did you have in mind?" Anne asked Michael suspiciously, ignoring Catherine's outburst.

Michael frowned thoughtfully. "It has to be something extraordinary," he murmured. "To convince you of what a jolly companion I am, so that leaves out a walk in the park. Anyone could take you there. I know!" he cried after a moment of silence. Turning to Catherine, he asked, "Have you seen much of London yet?"

"No, not a great deal," Catherine admitted cautiously.

"Then we must go to Astly's Amphitheatre," he announced.

Catherine looked blankly at Anne. "What is that?"

"It's a type of theater where they have horse shows," Anne explained without any show of enthusiasm. "They do put on an interesting show, but I doubt that we could get there in time for today's show."

"Of course we can," Michael insisted as he waved to a passing hackney. It passed him by, but there was another one close behind that came over to where they stood.

Catherine looked uncertainly at her two companions, worried by Anne's withdrawn manner. "Ought we to be going to a place like that?" she whispered to Anne.

Anne just shrugged. "Oh, it is perfectly respectable, if that's what you mean. But I do not know how enjoyable you will find it. It is just a few horses doing tricks in a circle."

Michael came back in time to hear Anne's last remark. Undaunted, he grinned at Catherine. "That is not what she said last year when I took her to see the show," he said. "She could not stop marveling about it."

Anne had the grace to blush, and followed Catherine and Michael over to the hackney. Michael handed Catherine up first, then took Anne's hand.

"I have to apologize for my outburst last night," she whispered stiffly.

Catherine looked at her in surprise, but Anne was staring at the ground. Michael only smiled gently as he squeezed her hand. "We had better hurry if we are to make the show."

Anne allowed him to help her into the carriage, then he climbed in also and sat across from the two girls. Sighing dramatically, he turned to Catherine. "It was all an elaborate plot, you know," he said to her confusion. "She chose to apologize now only because she wants me to spend the extra shilling to get us seats for the show instead of having to stand in the back."

Catherine smiled, and surprisingly, so did Anne, although hers seemed a trifle nervous. Anne did not speak, though, as they rode through the streets, but sat with her hands tightly clenched in her lap. She carefully kept her eyes downward except on the occasions when Michael pointed out some item of in-

147

terest to Catherine, then she would glance quickly at it also.

Catherine was enjoying their ride in spite of the nagging worry that she really ought to get back home. She also was very conscious of Anne's uneasiness, and sympathized with her. It must be very hard to be in the company of someone who looked like a lost love.

The carriage turned a corner suddenly, and Catherine fell slightly against Anne, but she barely noticed, for she had just realized what she had thought. If it was hard for Anne to be near Michael because he looked so like Edward, why was not it equally hard for her?

Catherine turned and pretended to be watching out the window, but actually saw none of the places they were passing. Michael's presence had bothered her yesterday, but only until she realized that it was not Edward come back to haunt her. If she had loved Edward, should not her reaction to Michael be more like Anne's? And last night, when Simon had made love to her, she had not felt any repulsion or even sadness that it was not Edward.

What kind of a love had she had for Edward? she wondered. Real love should not die that quickly. She glanced over at Anne and saw the tension and pain in her face. How was it that she was not suffering the same way? It was barely six months since Edward's death, and here she was, emotionally over the shock of his death, married to another man, and actually enjoying his lovemaking. There was

148

only one possible realization—she had not loved Edward.

Stunned by this sudden insight, Catherine was hardly aware that the carriage had stopped and Michael was waiting for her to get out. She smiled nervously around her, having almost forgotten where they were going, and was thankful that there were too many people bustling around for them to converse. Michael merely took their arms, and led them into the amphitheater.

"What do you mean, you did not find her?" Lord Killian snapped at the man sitting across the dirty table from him. "You have had a whole week. What have you been doing all this time?"

The other man shrugged, seemingly unconcerned by Lord Killian's anger. His whole body appeared languid, except his eyes, which were curiously active behind the curtain of filthy gray hair that fell over his forehead. It was doubtful that any movement, however slight, in the disreputable inn escaped his notice.

"They's a lot a inns in Lunnon," he said, and took a leisurely drink of his ale, then wiped his mouth with his sleeve. "And a lot of Mrs. Smiths."

"Are you sure that none of them are the one I want?" Lord Killian asked, trying not to lose his temper.

The man shook his head, then leaned back in his chair. "None a 'em was from ta colonies, but aye

149

think aye found a trace a 'er."

"Oh?"

Leaning forward again, the man glanced casually around him before speaking. "Aye think she wuz at the Royal George Inn last week."

"Last week?" Lord Killian cried. "What help is that now?"

"Thet was all aye could find." He shrugged. "She and her husband came from Southampton ta tha inn. They stayed one night and left. Weren't no more trace of 'em."

Lord Killian thoughtfully rested his chin in his hand. "So she does have someone else in this plot. I wonder how many other families she is planning on duping also," he murmured. After a long moment's silence he put down his hand and looked decisively at the man across from him. "Instead of searching further in London, I want you to go to Southampton. Find someone who was on that boat with her and learn anything you can about her, her companion, or her background. Anything and everything."

There was a long silence between the two men, then suddenly Lord Killian reached into a pocket inside his coat and pulled out a few coins. He tossed them on the table.

"That should cover the cost of getting there and back, and buying the liquor you might need to help someone's memory. Be back here in a week." He rose to his feet. "Bring me something I can use against her should she reappear, and there will be an extra twenty pounds in it for you."

Lord Killian did not wait for the man to agree or disagree with the arrangement, but turned and walked briskly from the inn.

"Is it not wonderful to have the family all together again?" Mrs. Bradford sighed. She looked up from her knitting as Madeline placed a cup of tea on the table next to her. "Thank you, my dear." She smiled.

Madeline forced herself to return the smile although she certainly did not share the older lady's enthusiasm. There was a bit too much family in the house for her liking, but she was wise enough not to let this attitude show.

After pouring her own cup of tea, Madeline picked it up and leaned back in her chair. "It is nice, though, to be able to have tea like this. Just the two of us," she admitted. "I certainly have missed our little talks these few days, although it sounds selfish to say," Madeline sighed. "There have been other people who needed you, so I must not begrudge them your company."

"Why, Madeline," Mrs. Bradford said, putting her knitting into her lap. "What a sweet thing to say."

Yes, was it not? Madeline thought as she smiled innocently.

"I had no idea you felt that way."

"Oh, yes," Madeline nodded with sincerity. "You know I was never close to my own mother. She had never seemed to care much about me, but these last few months I had begun to look upon you as the mother I wished I had. I do realize, too, with Simon and his family here now, you will be much busier and I am only glad that I had those early months with you."

"Why, you must not feel that I will forget about you, my dear," Mrs. Bradford assured her. "And with more young people in the house, you may find you prefer their company to mine."

Madeline smiled weakly and took a sip of her tea. "Yes, perhaps I shall." But her doubts were evident in her voice.

"Now, why must you say it that way?" the other lady scolded gently. "Simon's wife is lovely. You and she could be great friends."

Madeline put her tea down and looked wistfully across at Mrs. Bradford. "Yes, I had hoped so, but . . . maybe I am being silly . . . but she doesn't seem to like me very much."

"What nonsense! How can you say that?"

"Well, she and Anne went shopping today and did not ask me along."

"But you went out with Catherine last week and did not ask Anne along," Mrs. Bradford reminded her gently. "You must not let yourself be hurt by such things. You are too sensitive."

"Yes, that must be it," Madeline nodded with a brave smile. She picked up her tea and took a long drink. "I shall try not to be so silly."

Mrs. Bradford picked up her knitting again.

"Would you like me to speak with Catherine and Anne?"

"Oh, no." Madeline was horrified at the idea. "No, please do not. I would not want to force myself on them if they do not want my company."

"But I am sure that is not—"

"No, please do not. As long as you still like me and do not begin to exclude me also, I shall be happy."

"I would never exclude you. You are very special to me."

Madeline smiled in relief. "Would you like some more tea?" She was certain Bradleigh was in her reach.

Simon walked leisurely down Piccadilly, quite pleased with the way his business had gone. He had drawn up a new will so that Catherine would be well taken care of should something happen to him.

At the thought of his wife, Simon's step became a bit brisker. Even though he had made the decision to marry her rather impulsively, he certainly had not regretted it for a moment. She was kind, considerate, and loving, everything a man could want in a wife. He could not imagine himself married to anyone but her.

Simon stopped with a start. Catherine was the girl that he had dreamed Madeline was, he realized. And Madeline, well, she was best married to someone else. Starting to walk again slowly, Simon wondered if Madeline had not been married when he had returned, would he have rushed to marry her himself or would he have noticed that she was far different from the girl he had dreamed of. Luckily, he had not had to make that choice.

He crossed the street, and passed by Watiers, nodding to an acquaintance going inside. He had never had any desire to join that club in spite of the reputed excellence of its dinner table, since it was also reputed to be a place of deep purse, and Simon was not much of a gambler.

As he passed St. James's Street, he glanced down it toward the other two exclusive clubs in town, Whites and Brooks. He and Nigel were both members of Whites, but from what he had heard, he doubted that he would feel very comfortable there any longer. Apparently, in the last few years, Whites had been taken over by a very select group of dandies and they controlled the balloting of new members.

Simon had planned to walk up Bond Street and shop for a few little things he still needed, but as he was waiting to cross St. James's Street, he was hailed from behind.

"Simon? Simon Bradford?"

Simon turned around and was quite surprised to see Lord Killian addressing him. "Good day, my lord," Simon said calmly, successfully hiding his astonishment.

"I thought it was you, Simon," Lord Killian said as he held out his hand. "I heard you were back."

Simon gave his hand with a certain suspicion. He and Lord Killian had hardly been the best of friends when he had left for the army, so he wondered why the older man was actually stopping him on the street to speak.

"Were you on your way to one of the clubs?" Lord Killian asked. "You must have a drink with me to celebrate your return."

Even though Simon had no desire to go to any of the clubs, he was too astounded by Lord Killian's suggestions to refuse. Clearly the older man wanted something, and if Simon was patient enough, he would learn what it was. "I would be most honored to have a drink with you."

The two men walked down the street to Whites. Lord Killian said little as they entered the club and found seats in a nearby deserted sitting room. A waiter hurried over to ask what they would like to drink and a moment later returned with two brandies.

Lord Killian was sitting in a large leather-covered chair in a corner. He sniffed his brandy slowly, then took a small sip before carefully putting the glass down on a round table next to him. It was not until he folded his hands in his lap that he looked over at Simon, who was sitting a few feet away.

"Actually, Simon, I have considered speaking to you about this matter several times since I heard that you were back."

Simon's eyebrows rose slightly as he, too, put his glass down. "Yes?" he prompted.

Lord Killian shifted in his chair. "Did you ever see Edward when you were in Canada?"

Simon stared for a moment. This was not what he had expected. "Why, yes, I saw him once or twice over the last few years."

"Were you stationed in Halifax with him?"

Simon frowned. He remembered Madeline or his grandmother mentioning that Edward had been in Halifax for a time. "No, I was in Montreal," Simon said. "Occasionally, I was sent to Halifax, though, with dispatches and such."

"Then did you see him during this past year?"

"Yes, I believe so. In July or August."

Lord Killian impatiently waved aside Simon's hesitation. "The actual month does not matter," he quickly said. "The important thing is that you saw him, and when you did, did he mention any woman he was involved with?"

"A woman?" Simon shook his head. "No, I don't believe he did."

"There! I knew it was all a lie!" Lord Killian leaned back in his chair, a triumphant smile on his face.

"What was?"

"Some scheming hussy claimed that Edward had married her," Lord Killian said as he reached again for his brandy. "She actually expected that I would believe her Banbury tale."

He looked so pleased with himself, so certain that he was vastly superior to the rest of the mere mortals around him that Simon's stomach twisted with anger. "How do you know Edward didn't marry?" Simon asked.

Lord Killian had just taken a sip of the liquor and choked at Simon's question. "How do I know? Why, you just told me Edward was not married." Lord Killian's eyes flashed a warning that Simon disregarded.

Shaking his head quickly, Simon leaned forward in his chair. "No, I said that Edward did not mention it, but we spoke for only a few minutes," he pointed out. "And since he was betrothed to Anne, would he be likely to tell me anyway? I hardly think you can make a conclusion like that based on my short conversation with him."

"I am not basing it on what you've said," Lord Killian snapped. His voice was soft, deadly with menace, but strangely enough Simon was unmoved by it. "The devil!" Lord Killian went on. "If you had seen that shameless little piece, coming to me as bold as brass for money, you would have known she was lying too."

"Did you give her any money?" Simon asked curiously.

"Not a shilling!" Lord Killian admitted proudly. "No scullery maid is going to slumguzzle me, and I told her so. Edward might have taken a liking to her charms, but he would never have chosen some lightskirt to bear his children no matter what her fool piece of paper said."

Simon's eyes narrowed. "What kind of paper?" he asked curiously. "You mean she had marriage lines and you still did not believe she was married to Edward?"

"She had what she wanted me to believe were marriage lines," Lord Killian corrected himself. "But I am no fool. Hers were just some cheap copy so she could pretend her bastard had a name."

Simon frowned. "She had a child and you turned her away? What if Edward had married her? What if you turned away his child?" Simon asked.

With every word the man before him seemed to shrink in stature. Had Simon really once feared this man? Fear accords respect, though, and Lord Killian deserved none of that. He was cruel and petty, not a man to fear but to despise. Simon thought suddenly of Catherine and the cruel way she had been treated by her husband's family. He felt even more sickened at the thought of another young girl on her own in London, and got to his feet.

"If you will excuse me, Lord Killian," Simon said, his voice holding only the barest of civility. "But I must be getting on my way."

"You are as soft as an old woman," Lord Killian scoffed, obviously not fooled by Simon's meager pretense of courtesy. His lordship finished the rest of his drink and stood up also. "The next time Mrs. Smith comes to call, I shall send her to you since your heart bleeds for her so." He stalked away.

Simon's frown deepened along with his confusion. "Mrs. Smith?" he repeated dazedly though Lord Killian was already leaving the room and couldn't hear him. "But Edward's name was Corbett-Smith."

A sudden chaos of thoughts crowded his mind, jumbling and bumping one another until it seemed they were all shouting out the same impossible idea. Could Edward have been using only part of his name? Simon wondered. Could his Catherine have been married to Edward?

Totally dumfounded and feeling ready to gasp for air, Simon sank back into his chair. He felt confused, slow-witted, and addle-pated. As if someone had given him a leveler. Catherine and Edward! Was it possible? The more Simon thought about it, the more possible it became. She was from Halifax. Her husband had died around the same time as Edward, and she had been turned away by his family. And there was the matter of the name. Just too many pieces fit together for it to be a coincidence.

Simon was not sure how long he sat in the deserted sitting room in Whites. At first he was astonished at the thought that Catherine might have been Edward's wife, then he grew even angrier at the treatment she had received from Lord Killian. By the time he finished a second brandy, hurt nipped around the edges of his soul and a sadness tugged at his spirit. Why hadn't she told him the truth? Had she thought so little of him as to suppose that he would turn her away also?

Suddenly Simon was exhausted. He leaned back in his chair and closed his eyes, realizing only then why she had not told him the truth. Before they had married, she had no reason to believe that

Edward's name would mean anything to him, and considering the way Lord Killian had treated her, Simon could understand her reluctance to speak of Edward or his family at all. Then once she had met Madeline and Anne, she probably had not known how to tell him the truth. The question was, should he tell her he knew, or should he wait?

Chapter Nine

"I think I shall stay at home tonight," Mrs. Bradford announced during dinner. "Perhaps Simon or Catherine would be so kind as to give my excuses to the Lloyds."

Catherine looked up, wresting her thoughts from her afternoon with Michael and Anne. "Aren't you feeling well?" she asked Simon's grandmother.

"Oh, no," Mrs. Bradford said quickly. Her smile was bright as ever, and her eyes reassured them of the truth in her words. "I feel fine. I just thought that I would stay here and keep Madeline company." Her smile warmed as she glanced down the table at the young lady.

It was Nigel's turn to look confused. "Is she ill?" she asked.

"I am in mourning." Madeline's reprimand was gentle, shaming the others into a reminder of her loss.

But Nigel looked remarkably untouched by her soft scolding. "Ought to be half-mourning by now," he said offhandedly as a footman refilled his wineglass. After taking a sip, Nigel put the glass down and looked back at his grandmother. "I'm afraid I still don't understand what Madeline's mourning has to do with your attendance at the theater tonight."

"She thought I might appreciate some company while you all are out having fun," Madeline sighed with barely hidden impatience, then waved aside a footman who was bringing around the platter of beef for those who wanted more. "I do not see why everyone is making such a fuss about it."

"I hadn't realized that you found my company so boring," Anne noted, though Catherine could see that Simon's sister found Madeline's comments more amusing than insulting. "But, you know, Nigel is right," Anne went on. "It is more than six months since Edward's death, so we could go into half-mourning and start going about into society occasionally."

Madeline looked horrified, her face pale and her eyes reflecting pain. She rose to her feet, clenching her hands tightly before her. "You may go into half-mourning if you like," she told Anne. "But six months is not enough time to make me forget how much I loved my brother. And to join in the frivolities of society so soon after his death would seem like a mockery of everything he was." She wiped an invisible tear from her cheek and left the room.

Silence reigned for a long minute. Anne was staring down at her plate, her hands lying motionless on the table. She was lost in her own thoughts, and unaware of the fact that Catherine was watching her sympathetically. How like Madeline not to recognize anyone else's suffering, Catherine thought.

Nigel broke the spell when he tossed his napkin onto the table and picked up his wineglass. "Well, I would guess that my wife does not intend to accompany you to the theater tonight," he drawled sarcastically. "She does not intend to waste any of her tears on silly things like *Romeo and Juliet*." He took a long drink of his wine.

"She is right," Anne said quietly. "And it is wrong of you to mock her so. How can a silly play compare with the real tragedy of Edward's death?" After trying unsuccessfully to choke back a sob, Anne jumped to her feet and rushed from the room.

"My, my," Nigel said loudly. "It seems, Grandmother, that none of us need go to the theater tonight. We can get much more entertaining dramatics right here."

"Nigel," his grandmother scolded, then looked toward the door. "Poor Anne, I am certain that Madeline did not mean to criticize her. Perhaps I should go see how she is," she said as she rose to her feet.

"Please," Catherine cried, rising to her feet also. "Let me go to her." Without waiting for an answer, she turned and hurried after Anne.

Catherine found Anne in her bedroom, lying across her bed, sobbing brokenly into her pillow.

Catherine stood uncertainly just inside the door for a long moment, wondering what she could say or do that could comfort Anne. But the young woman's suffering was so acute, Catherine felt she had to do something.

Catherine walked across the room and sat on the edge of Anne's bed. "Anne, please do not cry so," she said gently as she touched the young woman's shoulder. "It will not help, you know."

Anne looked up from where she lay, her face streaked with tears and her eyes swollen and red. "I know," she cried, "but I can't seem to stop. I was betrothed to him. I had pledged to marry him, to spend the rest of my life with him. He went away to Canada believing I would be true to him. What kind of a person would betray that trust?"

Catherine took Anne's hand in hers and held it tightly. "But you are not betraying his trust," she tried to reason with Anne. "He would never have expected you to mourn him for the rest of your life just because you had been betrothed."

"Oh, you do not understand," Anne sobbed. She pulled her hand away from Catherine and walked over to her window to stare out at the darkness.

Catherine followed her. "I understand very well," she said. "I lost my father a month before Edward died. I loved him very much, but I could not devote the rest of my life to keeping his memory alive. I had to go on with my own life."

"It was different for you," Anne argued. "You had a husband and were going to have a baby. All I have are painful memories of broken promises. I cannot go anyplace without seeing Michael, and reliving all that hurt again." Her voice was bitter as she closed her eyes and leaned her forehead against the cool windowpane.

"You must stop it, Anne," Catherine said sharply. "You are young, and you will forget in time. You will meet someone who will help you forget."

Anne spun around, her face drained of color. "No!" she cried. "I can never forget! I owe Edward that much! The promises I made may be all useless now, but I can still honor his memory."

"Oh, Anne," Catherine sighed, not knowing what to say. Anne turned back to the window, tears sliding silently down her cheeks.

Although Anne seemed much calmer, Catherine could sense the pain she was feeling. Still, Catherine knew there were times when a person needed to be alone to cry, so after giving Anne a quick hug, she slipped from her room.

Simon was waiting in their room when Catherine went in. "How is Anne?" he asked.

Catherine shrugged her shoulders wearily. "I am not certain that I was able to help her," she said. "I did not know what to say." She sat down on the edge of the bed.

Simon came over to sit next to her and took her hand. "It must have been very hard for you, considering the circumstances."

"The circumstances?"

"Yes." Simon nodded. "You losing your husband

so close to the time that Anne lost her fiancé."

He paused, almost as if he were waiting for her to admit that the two people actually were the same, but of course that was ridiculous. Just her own nervous thoughts trying to find peace. She stood up and walked across to her dressing table to examine some combs.

"I did not tell her that, of course," Catherine said over her shoulder. "I did mention my father's death, but I do not think she found any consolation in what I said. She wants to mourn for him."

Simon walked over to where she stood and, after watching her play with the combs, he reached over and took her hand, letting a comb fall to the floor.

"That is something I cheated you of," he said quietly. "I took away your chance to mourn for your husband, and I am sorry."

Catherine looked up at him and shook her head slightly. "I think offering Teddy and me a home was more considerate than allowing me to mourn publicly for my husband while we both starved to death."

"I am fortunate you are so understanding," Simon said with a smile as he pulled her into his arms.

He kissed her lips gently, a soft, promising touch that almost seemed to ask her to trust him. But she just let her head rest against his chest, wishing she would confide in him but not wanting to risk what she had.

"So, tell me," Simon said after a minute. "Are we

going to the theater with the Lloyds, or shall we stay home?"

Catherine pulled away from him reluctantly. "Oh, I guess we should go," she sighed.

"That does not sound particularly enthusiastic," Simon laughed. "But I think we ought to go if you feel up to it." Catherine looked puzzled as he went on. "As much as I would like to, we could hardly retire for the evening right now." He leaned forward and kissed the tip of her nose as she blushed. "And I would just as soon not sit around watching Madeline and Anne try to be more mournful than the other."

Catherine laughed. "I shall change then."

The Lloyds were a pleasant couple in their late forties with eight children, although six of them were already married with children of their own. Mrs. Lloyd was a friendly woman by nature and filled with motherly advice which she dispensed frequently.

"I cannot imagine how you did it, my dear!" she exclaimed to Catherine as they chatted during the first intermission. Mr. Lloyd had left their box to get glasses of lemonade for them, while his wife talked to Simon and Catherine. "I would be petrified just to sail across to France, but to actually sail from Canada with a tiny infant! It just befuddles my mind!"

"It really was not all that difficult," Catherine

laughed.

"Not difficult?" the older woman echoed faintly. "In March, with all the storms? It must have been ghastly! Simon, you should be horsewhipped for making your wife and son sail then."

Simon smiled and reached over to take Catherine's hand. "We were eager to get home," he said.

"You mean *you* were eager to get home," Mrs. Lloyd corrected Simon with a snort of derision. "Men always think of what they want."

Catherine laughed softly at the look of surprise on Simon's face. He was not certain if Mrs. Lloyd's attack was serious. "It was my idea to leave Canada then too," she said, coming to Simon's defense.

"Well, you are braver than I am," the older lady said with a shudder. "Now, you must tell me how you met," she said eagerly.

Catherine and Simon exchanged startled glances.

"I can tell it must have been terribly romantic," Mrs. Lloyd said excitedly. "Did you fall in love with her the first moment you saw her?" she asked Simon.

Catherine bit back a laugh as she remembered their first meeting, and glanced up at Simon in amusement. He returned her glance, and his eyebrows rose when he saw the humor in her face. A wicked gleam came into his eyes.

"I do not know how you guessed it, but I did," he said quite seriously. "The moment I set eyes on her, I was in love." He saw Catherine's lips twitch

168

slightly as he went on. "Whenever I was near her, the ground seemed to pitch and roll, and I could actually hear a little voice—that must have been my heart—crying out for her."

"Oh, my, that is lovely," Mrs. Lloyd sighed. "It is so wonderful to hear a young couple admit that they care about each other when so many people marry just for convenience." She leaned a little closer to them. "I would like to know what is so convenient about being married to someone you detest?" she asked.

"That is an excellent point," Simon agreed. He brought Catherine's hand up to his lips and kissed it gently as he smiled into her eyes. "And I am so lucky that it is a point I need never worry about."

Catherine blushed a vivid red at the implication of his words as Mr. Lloyd came back into the box.

"Had a little trouble with one of the glasses," he apologized as he handed Catherine and his wife a glass. "Some fool bumped into me and spilled it."

"On himself?" Mrs. Lloyd asked.

He nodded with a grin. "Served him right for being so clumsy." He looked over at Simon. "I'll go back and get another glass," he said.

Simon stood up. "No, don't be silly. I can go. You stay here and relax before the next act starts." Simon squeezed Catherine's hand before he let go of it, and left the box.

"Well, you are a popular young lady," Mr. Lloyd told her after he took a drink of his lemonade. "Several people stopped me in the hallway to ask who was the lovely young lady in our box." He winked at his wife. "I think they were looking for some tasty gossip."

Mrs. Lloyd smiled at Catherine. "We are lucky that we asked you to the theater so soon after your arrival. Before we know it, you will be sitting with the dukes and duchesses and forgetting us common folk."

"Oh, never," Catherine denied with a smile.

"Do not be too quick to argue," Mr. Lloyd warned in a friendly way. "One of the people who asked who you were was none other than Lord Killian!"

"Lord Killian!" Catherine gasped. She could feel herself go pale, but hoped that the theater was too shadowy for anyone to notice. "He saw me?"

Mr. Lloyd nodded as a commotion from below them indicated that the second act was about to begin. "And he is quite choosy about whom he associates with," he added.

Catherine's mouth went dry. She turned slightly in her chair so that she was facing the stage more directly, but she actually was searching through the audience for a certain forbidding face. She didn't catch a glimpse of him, but that only made her fears grow. He wouldn't confront her here, would he?

She felt Simon return to his seat and forced herself to turn back toward him, smiling slightly. Luckily, the play had begun and talking was impossible, but so was concentration for her. She had no idea what was happening onstage and rather kept seeing her own little drama, complete with a sinister villain, playing out their parts in her mind. Then the second act was over, and before Catherine had any time to compose herself, Simon was smiling at her and making some inane comment. She just stared blankly at him.

"Catherine," he asked. "Is something wrong?"

Only that her sweet little interlude was about to be shattered. Fighting an urge to burst into tears, she tried to make some excuse for her behavior. "I do not feel very well," she whispered. She raised one hand to rub her forehead, but it was trembling so badly that she quickly put it back in her lap. "I . . . I have a headache," she said lamely.

Simon looked so concerned that Catherine tried to smile reassuringly. Somehow she had to make it through the rest of the play.

"Would you like to leave?" he asked quietly. "I am certain the Lloyds will not mind."

"Is something wrong?" Mrs. Lloyd had noticed how pale Catherine was, and suddenly it was out of her control. "Are you not well, child?"

Her sympathy was almost Catherine's undoing. The tears that had been threatening began to roll slowly down her cheeks as Catherine shook her head. She tried to wipe them away inobtrusively, but Mrs. Lloyd noticed.

"I think it would be best if you took her home, Simon," she said.

"I am so sorry," Catherine murmured.

"Now, now, you must not be," Mrs. Lloyd assured her. "I know just what the problem is."

"You do?" Catherine asked.

Mrs. Lloyd nodded. "It is that ocean voyage catching up with you. All you need is some rest. You are just trying to do too much too soon."

Catherine smiled slightly. "You are very kind," she said. "I am sorry to spoil the evening for you."

"Nonsense, you just go home with your husband, and in a few days, when you are feeling better, you can invite us for tea," Mr. Lloyd said.

"We shall," Simon promised, and wrapping Catherine's shawl around her shoulders, he led her out of the box.

Catherine was never certain how she kept the tears back as Simon led her through the halls of people. She prayed the whole time that they would not meet up with Lord Killian, and breathed a sigh of relief once they were outside waiting for the carriage.

"We will be home soon," Simon said. He was being so kind and considerate that Catherine felt like a fraud, but she could not tell him about Edward while they were standing out in the street or during the short carriage ride home.

Once they reached his grandmother's home, the footman was in the hallway, and she could hear voices from the sitting room. She looked in exasperation at the large clock near the stairs. It was not late enough for anyone to have retired.

"Go up to your room," Simon told her. "I'll send

your maid up to—"

"No," she cried. Sensing that the footman had turned toward her, she lowered her voice. "No," she said in a whisper. "Please, Simon, I have to talk to you." She blinked away the tears that were forming again.

"Simon? Are you back already?" Anne called from the sitting room. There was the sound of footsteps approaching the hallway.

Simon glanced toward the sitting room door, and then back at Catherine. "Go on up," he told her. "I shall make some excuses and be up soon."

She nodded, for tears were making speech impossible, and hurried up the stairs. It was not until she closed the bedroom door behind her that she finally felt safe. By that time the tears were coming so fast that there was no way she could stop them. She walked over to the soft rug before the fireplace, threw herself onto it, resting her head in her arms on the seat of a chair, and sobbed her heart out.

How had she thought that she would get away with her deception? True, she hadn't intended to deceive Simon when she married him, but would that matter when compared to the heartache her presence would soon cause?

Simon had been so good to her, so considerate and concerned, and all she was going to bring him was trouble. Why is it that the ones who cause all the trouble were never the ones to suffer?

Catherine had not heard Simon come into the room, but suddenly he was there, lifting her up into his arms, and holding her close while she cried. After a time the tears began to slow, and she pulled slightly away from him, wiping her face with the back of her hand.

Simon took a snowy white handkerchief from his pocket and gently wiped the traces of the tears from her cheeks. It was then that she realized that she was sitting in his lap in the chair before the fireplace. She tried to slip away from him, from the comfort his arms promised, but he would not let her.

"Now, tell me what is wrong," he said.

With him sitting so close to her, Catherine did not know what to say. She could not look him in the face and tell him the truth, but she had to!

"You are not sick, are you?" he prodded gently.

She shook her head. "No, I am not," she whispered. "But I have to tell you something and I do not know how." She tried again to move off his lap. If she could just get away from him slightly, she could tell him, she thought frantically, but his arms still held her tight.

"It will not make it any easier if you move away," he said. He pushed her head back onto his chest and leaned back in the chair himself. She felt loved and protected in his arms now, but what would he do when he knew the truth?

"Now," Simon continued. "What is this terrible thing that you have to tell me? Is it about Edward?"

His words were so unexpected that they seemed to knock the breath from her body. She sat up in his arms, staring into his eyes. "You knew?" she whispered. "You knew all this time?"

"No." He shook his head and pulled her back into his arms. "I found out this afternoon when I accidentally met Lord Killian."

"Oh, Lord," she moaned softly, and buried her face in his coat.

His arms tightened around her. "He did not know who my wife was, of course, but it did not take me long to see that there were too many coincidences between you and the woman he was speaking of."

She lay there a moment, torn between the agony of Simon's knowing and the wonder that she was still in his arms. Might the situation be not quite as hopeless as she had feared?

"I was upset at first that you did not tell me yourself, but I do understand," Simon said gently. "You loved him, and were not ready to talk about him yet."

"No!" Catherine cried. The truth, the real truth had to be told. She pulled away from him and looked into his face. "I hated him. He thought my father had money, but when he learned the truth, I rarely saw him. He never told his family about me, and probably never meant to bring me back with him. I was too ashamed to tell you the truth and too afraid that you would not believe me."

"Why wouldn't I believe you?" Simon demanded. "Don't you think I trust you?"

Catherine sighed. "But the way Madeline and Anne speak of him . . ."

Simon let out his breath slowly. "Anne, yes," he said. "She's taking his death much harder than I would have thought. To me, Edward was always too high in the instep to be even tolerable." Catherine felt her heart slow, just beginning to allow her to relax as she lay back in his arms. Simon seemed almost unaware that she had moved. "I never could understand why others seemed to idolize him so."

"He could be very charming," Catherine noted quietly.

Simon looked down at her. "Yes, I suppose he must have been at some time, or you would not have married him."

Neither of them spoke for some time. Catherine felt exhausted now that she had finally told him the truth, and wonderfully wanted in his arms, but a few things still nagged at her.

"Lord Killian saw me at the theater tonight," she said suddenly. "He asked Mr. Lloyd who I was."

"So that is what caused the problem," Simon said. "I wondered why you had suddenly decided to confide in me."

Catherine said nothing for a moment. "I wanted to tell you long ago," she said quietly.

"I know." He bent down and kissed her forehead. "What will Lord Killian do now?"

"What can he do?" Simon shrugged. "We are legally married, and you were legally married before. If he tells anyone about you and Edward, he will have to reveal his treatment of you, and that would hardly make him look good. Now that he knows you will make no further claim on him as Edward's wife, I do not imagine he will do anything."

"I hope you are right," she sighed.

"You have to have a little more faith in me," he teased her gently. He put his hand under her chin and made her look up into his eyes. "You are my wife now, remember? I will not let him do anything that would hurt you."

"Oh, Simon." She sighed again as she slid her arms around his neck. "Love me. Just love me."

He bent down slowly to kiss her, tasting the salt from her tears on her lips. She clung to him desperately, needing the reassurance of his love that she was safe.

Last night he had been gentle in his lovemaking, but tonight he was rougher, less carefully controlled. He sensed that she needed to respond to him fully, that in order to rid them of Edward's ghost, he had to make her understand that she truly belonged in his arms.

While his hands slowly ran down her back, he kissed her deeply, awakening in her a deep hunger that she'd never known before. The stars seemed to be glittering in his eyes and the songs of the heavens seemed to echo in her heart. This was love, she thought, this was real belonging. The smile on his lips came from his soul, she knew, and seemed to burst alive into sunshine inside her. There was no anger in his face, nothing but love and tenderness in his touch.

Her feelings for Edward had been a ghost, a

shadowy echo of real cherishing, and she let them fade away in the night without a protest. Simon was everything she wanted and needed; their life together would be beyond the wildest dancing dreams of her heart. It would be magic.

"Oh, Kate," he sighed as he looked down into her eyes. "You belong with me. Don't you see that? Nothing else matters except that we found each other."

"No, nothing else does matter," she answered as his lips came down to crush hers, and she was lost in a blur of their love.

Chapter Ten

"Good morning, Mrs. Marley." Kendall bowed as he stepped aside to let Madeline into her father's house. "Are you here to see anyone in particular?"

Madeline scowled at the man. "I am here to see my father," she informed him curtly, pushing past him and going into the library. It was cold and empty.

The butler followed along behind her. "I am not certain his lordship has arisen," Kendall said hesitantly.

Madeline pulled open a pair of drapes with an impatient jerk, and spun around to face the butler. "Of course he is up," she argued. "He sent for me, and he could hardly do that if he was asleep, could he?"

"No, certainly not, madam," he murmured, and backed out of the room. "Shall I bring you some tea?" he asked from the doorway.

"Just get my father, will you?" Madeline snapped. The butler nodded and quietly closed the door behind him. Madeline looked around her for a moment, then sank into a chair near her father's desk. A clock on the mantel chimed nine, and she glared up at it. Nine o'clock in the morning was a ghastly time to be up and about, but she could hardly ignore a summons from her father, especially when it sounded as urgent as this one had.

The door opened suddenly, and Lord Killian strode in. "Ah, Madeline, my dear," he cried happily. "You are just the person I wanted to see."

Madeline stared at him in surprise, for he had never greeted her like this before. She was further astonished when he placed a hand on each of her shoulders and bent down to kiss her cheek.

"And how are you this morning?" he went on. Still holding one of her hands, he sat down in a nearby chair.

"I am fine," she murmured, staring at him in surprise.

"Ah, I only wish I could say the same about myself," her father sighed.

"Why, whatever is wrong?" Madeline felt a chill settle around her heart. "Are you ill?"

"No, no." He shook his head slowly. After squeezing her hand gently, he let go of it and stood up. "I only wish it were something that simple," he said as he walked restlessly around the room.

It was not like her father to confide his troubles to her, but Madeline decided to probe a little further. She longed for the chance to make her father proud of her, even if she was not his heir.

"Please come back and sit down," she suggested softly. "Maybe if you told me about it . . ."

Surprisingly, her father did come back to his chair. "Something dreadful has happened, and I do not know how to tell you. I do not even know if I should tell you," he added. "What good will it do for you to be upset also?"

Madeline reached over to take his hand. "Of course you must tell me. Perhaps together we might think of a solution."

Lord Killian sighed, and seemed to give in. "It is about Edward," he began. "A few weeks ago a woman came to me, claiming to have been his wife."

"His wife!" Madeline cried. "He had married?"

"Of course not," her father snapped impatiently. "His letters never mentioned a wife. In fact, much the opposite. They were full of his plans for marriage to Anne."

Madeline nodded knowingly. "So what did this woman want?"

Lord Killian raised his eyebrows in surprise. "What do you think she wanted? Money, of course. She had hoped that I would be stupid enough to agree to support her and her brat."

"There was a child? Edward had a child?" Madeline whispered.

Her father glared at her. "Are you that naive?" he asked sarcastically. "With a woman like that, anyone could be the brat's father. There was no way that she could prove it was Edward's. We are a well-known family, with considerable assets. This young woman most probably knew Edward, and thought that if she came forward after his death when he could not deny it and said they were married, I would be fool enough to believe her. She must have hoped that I would welcome her into the family with open arms, and provide her with the funds to lead a comfortable existence." ·

"She must have been incredibly stupid to think that she could fool you or anyone without any proof," Madeline noted.

Lord Killian shrugged his shoulders. "Oh, she was not that foolish. She had some obvious forgery that she hoped to pass off as her marriage lines, but I was not tricked. I sent her packing like the cheap baggage she was."

"You should have had her thrown into prison," Madeline cried. "The impudence of the little hussy, besmirching Edward's memory like that!" Madeline quietly fumed for a few minutes. Suddenly she looked up at her father. "Why are you still upset? You ruined her little plan, so why aren't you delighted?"

"Oh, I was for a few days," her father agreed in a moment of rare honesty. "But then I began to worry about those marriage lines. I knew they were false, but supposing she went to some unscrupulous lawyer and convinced him they were real?"

"She could cause a nasty scandal."

"The scandal would be unimportant next to what else she could do," he pointed out. "With a conniving lawyer behind her, she could take those false marriage lines to court and force us to recognize her as Edward's widow."

"Legally recognize perhaps."

"Don't you see? If she is recognized as Edward's widow, then that makes her son Edward's heir. And my heir," Lord Killian cried.

"Oh, my," Madeline breathed in horror. The full import of what her father said finally sank in. "What in the world can we do? Have you told Michael?"

Her father shook his head impatiently. "Edward and I were very much alike," he said with a sigh. "I think that you, my dear, are also a lot like us." Madeline sat up a little straighter at the compliment. "But Michael has always been different. He has never understood what it means to be a Killian. He would be all too likely to hand over his inheritance to that fool chit."

Madeline nodded sympathetically. "You can depend on me though," she promised. "If there is anything that I can do for you, just tell me."

Lord Killian patted her hand and smiled gratefully at her. "As it happens, you are in an excellent position to help. You see, when I began to worry about those lines, I had no idea where the chit was, but now I know."

"She is still in London, then?" Madeline asked.

"Oh, yes," her father nodded. "Apparently up to some new slumguzzling, but still dangerous to us, nevertheless."

183

"And there is something I can do to stop her?" Madeline asked eagerly.

"You must get those lines from her," her father said quietly. "Without that piece of forgery, she is no threat to us. Edward's memory would be safe." Madeline nodded solemnly. "If she was to have another one made, it would be much easier to prove false since she would have to have it done here in England."

"But how could I get those lines?" Madeline asked in bewilderment. "Surely she has them in a safe place, and how would I get the chance to search for them? I could not slip into someone's house unnoticed, even if I happened to be acquainted with this woman, as unlikely as that seems."

"That is where you are wrong, my dear." Lord Killian smiled unpleasantly. "Not only are you acquainted with the lady in question, you also live in the same house with her."

Madeline frowned thoughtfully as she tried to remember if they had a new maid in the house. There were some new faces working in the nursery, she realized.

"You see," Lord Killian went on. "This woman who claimed to be your brother's wife now claims to be married to Simon Bradford!"

"And what plans do you two have for today?" Mrs. Bradford asked as she looked across the breakfast table at Catherine and Simon.

Catherine had no real plans, her newly discovered happiness too precious to think of trivial items like planning her day. Simon spoke for her.

"I had thought we might take a drive down to Bradleigh for the day," he said. A footman brought over his breakfast—a juicy steak just broiled along with a liberal portion of eggs. Simon nodded his thanks and began to eat.

"You are going down there just for the day?" his grandmother asked. "It seems like a very long day for Catherine." She looked with concern at her. "It is a lovely drive, but do you feel up to it, my dear?"

Catherine nodded. The idea of seeing Simon's home was appealing, but not as appealing as the idea of spending the day with him. "Oh, yes, I would love to see it. Although I had thought it was too far to visit in one day."

Mrs. Bradford shook her head with a smile. "Actually, I envy you. The countryside is so lovely this time of year . . ."

"Then why not join us?" Simon invited.

Anne had entered the room in time to hear Simon's invitation. "Oh, no," she laughed. "Grandmother already had plans for today, as much as she would like to forget them."

Mrs. Bradford looked slightly put out. "I was not going to accept their invitation," she said. "As much as the idea of a day in the country appealed to me."

"What are you doing today?" Catherine asked.

She had toyed with her food, feasting more on Simon's smile than on eggs and ham, then finally had pushed her plate away.

"We are going to visit Cousin Theodora," Anne said as she sat down next to Catherine. A footman poured her tea while another carried in a plate of freshly baked muffins and put them down before the young women.

"Who is Cousin Theodora?" Catherine asked. She turned to Simon. "I had not realized that you had more relations that I had not met."

Anne took one of the muffins and broke it in half. "She is more Grandmother's relative than ours," she noted as she took a bite of warm muffin. "And actually a recluse."

"Not that she has to be," Mrs. Bradford interrupted. "But she had a silly fight with Sally Jersey four years ago, and refused to go out into society until Sally apologized."

"And she did not?" Catherine asked with a smile.

"Who could blame her?" Mrs. Bradford shrugged with a laugh. "Actually, Theodora was something of a wet fish, and not exactly an asset to a party. However, she demands to be kept up-to-date on all the gossip, so I visit her a few times a month while we are in town."

Anne washed down her muffin with a drink of tea. "Today I have been summoned along, but I will wager that she will demand to see you next," Anne told Catherine.

"I think we can survive her inquisition." Simon

laughed.

"No, it is the tea she serves that is hard to survive," Mrs. Bradford said. She wiped her mouth with her napkin and rose to her feet. "Are you finished, Anne? We might as well be on our way."

Anne nodded without much enthusiasm and drained the last of her tea from her cup. Then she, too, stood up. "I hope you two can still enjoy yourselves, knowing what drudgery Grandmother and I are suffering," she teased.

"We shall do our best to put it out of our minds," Simon promised. His eyes found Catherine's and promised that the day would be filled with sunshine, not shadows.

Anne made a face at her brother, and followed her grandmother from the room. As she left, Nigel entered and looked around him with a frown.

"Have any of you seen Madeline?" he asked.

Catherine shook her head, generous in her happiness and wishing it for others, even Madeline. "No, I have not," she said. "But she's not usually downstairs at this time of the morning."

"Apparently, she rose earlier than normal today," Nigel noted. He stood by the sideboard, deep in thought, as his fingers tapped impatiently on the wooden surface next to him.

"Might aye get ya somethin', sir?" a footman inquired politely.

Nigel appeared slightly startled by his presence. "No, no." He waved the man away. "I never have breakfast. You must know that."

187

The footman bowed and left the room, while Nigel walked slowly over to the table and sat down in the place vacated by his grandmother.

Catherine watched him sympathetically. Although to her Madeline did not seem particularly dependable, it was obvious that Nigel was concerned by her unexplained absence. Catherine wished there were something she could say to ease his mind, but her opinions of Madeline's selfish nature would hardly make him feel better.

"We are going to ride out to Bradleigh today," Simon said, interrupting her thoughts. "Can we do anything for you while we are there?"

Nigel looked over at her and nodded. "Yes, I have some papers that you could give to Laughton. He's managing the estate now," he added. "And could take you about and show you some of the improvements I have made."

"Yes, Grandmother has told of some of them, and I certainly would like to see them for myself," Simon agreed.

Before he could say more, the dining room door opened and Madeline sauntered in. She yawned delicately, covering her mouth with her hand, and walked over to her place at the table.

"I thought I would come down for breakfast today," she said, and smiled at the others. "Although I fear I shocked my maid with the suggestion. She firmly believes that all proper ladies remain in bed until at least noon." She laughed quietly.

A footman brought her cup of hot chocolate and

dished up a plate of eggs and crisp bacon from the sideboard for her.

"How fortunate we are that you managed to escape her clutches." Nigel leaned back in his chair, his tone mocking.

Madeline looked up at him, her eyes innocently questioning his sarcasm.

"I think we had better be on our way," Simon said suddenly. He rose to his feet and held out his hand to Catherine.

"I will get those papers for you in a moment," Nigel said, but he made no attempt to stand. He just continued to watch Madeline.

"No hurry," Simon said quickly. "We are not quite ready to leave." He took Catherine's arm and led her from the room.

Madeline watched them leave with a friendly smile that faded as the door swung closed behind them. "Are they going somewhere?" she asked casually.

"To Bradleigh for the day," Nigel said. His eyes never left Madeline's face.

Quite aware of Nigel's close scrutiny, Madeline smiled back at him and began to eat. She successfully hid her sudden rage at the thought of that vulgar, scheming hussy visiting her estate. That despicable woman had no right to go there! Her very presence would desecrate the land that was once, and would again be, part of the Killian estate! But Madeline did not give her thoughts away. She merely smiled innocently, and said, "It looks like a lovely day to drive into the country."

"Oh?" Nigel feigned surprise. "And how can you tell? Did your maid allow you to look out the window?"

Madeline forced herself to smile, realizing that it was foolish to pretend that she just awakened. "Actually, I went for a short walk this morning before I came in here," she admitted. "It seemed like such a lovely morning, I hated to waste it all staying inside the house."

Nigel was openly cynical. "Ah, yes, I can well imagine it. Striding briskly along the streets, taking deep breaths of the fresh morning air. It does seem like you."

"If you must know, I stopped in at Father's house for a moment," she sniffed.

"The devil! Not another crying session over the death of the godly Edward."

Nigel sounded disgusted, and Madeline could no longer hold her impatience in check. "I will not have you speaking of him that way!" she cried. "He was a wonderful person. You could never be anything like him."

Nigel said nothing for a moment, but rose slowly to his feet, and walked around the table toward his wife. Madeline felt a twinge of apprehension as she sensed his anger, but she continued to hold her head up high.

"What a pity, then, that you married me," Nigel said, taking hold of her wrist. "But marry me you did, and I think it is about time that you concerned

190

yourself more with me than with your father or your dead brother." Although his voice was quiet, the words were said with deadly certainty.

"You do not understand." Madeline's will wavered, but she kept her eyes on him.

"I understand only too well." His voice was quiet, but ringing with the irony in it. "Your father's overrated sense of importance made Edward into an egotistical, selfish boor."

"No!" Madeline cried.

Ignoring her, Nigel went on. "Now that he is dead, and, I suspect, Michael refuses to assume his affectations, your father has suddenly remembered his adoring daughter."

"You are wrong," Madeline said. Her heart wanted to stop, her hands clenched as she jerked her arm away from him. "You are wrong."

Nigel's anger seemed to have faded. "Am I? Your father cares only about himself, and if you believe anything else, you are a fool."

Madeline forced herself to breathe evenly, to still the pounding in her temples. "I hate you! I should never have married you."

Surprisingly, Nigel found this amusing. "Quite possibly so," he agreed. "But you did, and do not expect me to share you much longer with your dead brother. I am beginning to think I should like a family."

"Like Simon and his loving wife?" she mocked. "Do not expect me to follow you about with such soulful eyes."

"Oh, but I do." He laughed unpleasantly as his hand lightly stroked her cheek. His smile broadened when she tried to pull away. "I shall expect, no—demand—that you be the devoted wife for all to see."

"And just how shall you force me to play such a part? For I certainly would not do so willingly."

Nigel smiled and turned to the door. "I shall not have to force you, my dear. Someday soon you will realize that I am the only one who truly cares what happens to you. You will be quite happy to become a loving wife."

"Never!"

Nigel only smiled and went out the door.

Madeline glared at the closed door for several minutes, then sank slowly back into her chair. How dare he say such things about her father and Edward! She had been right, she never should have married him. It would have been so much simpler to have waited until Simon returned and then marry him. He had always been much easier to manipulate.

Pushing her half-eaten breakfast away from her, Madeline smiled unpleasantly. She would have her revenge on this whole simple-minded family and she would get Bradleigh. With what her father had told her that morning, she had the right weapons to fight them all. She just had to wait for the right moment.

Hearing noises in the foyer below her, Madeline left the room. She walked silently to the top of the stairs and peered down. Catherine and Simon were leaving and Nigel was seeing them off. Smiling to herself, she drew back so that she would not be seen. Soon Nigel would also leave the house to go to his clubs or wherever he spent his day. She would be free to pursue her own interests.

The small sitting room that Madeline used was at the front of the house and gave her a clear view of everyone leaving and entering. She went to the room, but was too tense to sit and relax. Instead, she paced restlessly back and forth, going over in her mind all the things her father had told her. She let her anger build against Catherine and everyone who thought she was so wonderful.

She had disliked Catherine from the beginning, Madeline told herself proudly. She had not been fooled by her seemingly modest and unassuming ways. It was true she had not guessed just how truly despicable Catherine was, but she had never met anyone truly wicked before.

Madeline stopped at the window and looked down at Simon and Catherine as their carriage pulled away from the house. She watched a moment longer, but did not see Nigel leave also, so she continued her restless walking.

The mild dislike that she had initially felt for Catherine had grown into real hatred that morning. The fact that she had tried to get money from some innocent family by pretending to have been married to their deceased son was bad enough, but to have chosen Edward and their family as her victims was

193

terrible. She had tried to use Edward's death for her gain, not caring how she debased his memory in the eyes of those who loved him.

Madeline closed her eyes and shivered at the thought. There was no way that she could adequately make Catherine pay for what she had tried to do, but she would not rest until Catherine was punished. She would make certain that everyone knew what kind of a woman Simon's "perfect little wife" was.

Another noise from the front of the house sent her hurrying to the window. Nigel was leaving at last. She watched him walk down the street and around a corner. She was alone in the house with the servants now, for Mrs. Bradford and Anne had left earlier. It was the perfect time to find those false marriage lines.

With a pleasant smile Madeline left the sitting room and strolled leisurely up the stairs. Several maids were bustling about, cleaning rooms and changing the bed linens. They curtsied respectfully when they saw her.

Madeline nodded in return as she went straight to Catherine's room. She opened the door and let herself inside.

For a moment she stood just inside the door and looked around. She had been in the room before, but not since Simon and Catherine had moved into it. Somehow she had not expected it to hold so much of their presence.

Although their clothes were put away, Catherine's

lilac scent lingered in the air. Combs and brushes lay on the dressing table, partially covered by a pair of white gloves that had been tossed on top. Simon's cane was leaning against the side of the small writing desk, while its chair stood at an angle as if someone had just gotten up from it.

Madeline felt a slight twinge of uneasiness as she took a step forward. She had not expected the room to seem so personal.

She must not be so silly, she scolded herself. She must remember what that woman tried to do, and what she still might do: take Bradleigh away from her.

Her nerve strengthened, Madeline crossed the room purposefully. She had no idea where Catherine might have put the paper, but decided to begin with the dressing table.

She pulled open the top drawer. It was filled with ribbons and combs and other hair trim. Madeline searched through it quickly but found nothing hidden there.

The other two drawers held nothing of value either. There was a small jewel casket in one that had a worthless gold locket and some tarnished ivory combs, but there were no papers. Under some shawls she found a red leather folder and pulled it out hopefully, but it contained only some unused writing paper and two worn quills.

Madeline opened the wardrobe in the corner of the room. There were not many clothes hanging in it, and it did not take long to see that nothing else

195

was hidden there.

The small desk held an assortment of anonymous writing paper and sealing waxes that had probably been there for years. She closed the drawer with a frown. Where the devil could she have hidden that piece of paper?

The noise of the maids in the next room warned Madeline that she must not stay much longer. Think, she scolded herself, think. Where could it be?

Since it could well be damaging if found, Catherine would hide it very well. In a safe if there was one. No, she thought quickly, Simon would have had to open it for her and then he would have seen it. Disgusted as Madeline was with him, she could not believe he was involved in Catherine's little schemes. No, he was just another of her victims.

As Madeline glanced around the room again, her eyes stopped on the wardrobe and she walked slowly toward it. She pulled the door open again, and stared at the dresses. They were all new, she realized, and quickly looked through the drawers again. It was the same. Everything was new. Had she gotten rid of everything she had before? It seemed unlikely, so she must have put her old things away.

Madeline hurried from the room and, picking up a candlestick from a table nearby, hurried up the next flight of stairs. She went past the servants' floor and into the attics.

They were very dark, even with her candle, and it

took a few minutes for her eyes to become accustomed to the dark. Once they had, she frowned at all the clutter. There were piles and piles of old dusty furniture and discarded portraits.

Holding her dress up so that it did not pick up dust from the floor, Madeline edged slowly around the things stored up there. Few trunks were in evidence, so she went into the next room.

This one had at least a dozen trunks and most were so dusty, it was obvious they had not been touched for years. Next to the far wall, however, were several newer ones, and she hurried toward them.

The first two were her own, and the next had Anne's initials on the front. One beyond them was quite battered, and she tugged hopefully at the closure, only to find it was locked.

Madeline could have sworn with frustration and glanced around for something to force the lock with. It was then she saw another trunk pushed up against the far wall. It was obviously new also, but had a different look to it. Could it be because it was made in Canada?

She hurried over to it and knelt down, forgetting her desire to protect her clothing. It was unlocked! She opened the clasp and pushed back the top. The first thing that caught her eye was a piece of blue silk—the dress Catherine had worn that first day.

Madeline quickly pushed the dresses aside and searched through the trunk. Besides the old clothing, there were several boxes of various shapes and sizes. One had letters in it, another some cheap jewelry, and the third, a yellowed shawl. Madeline sighed in discouragement. It had to be here.

Under the last box she had opened Madeline found a small bundle wrapped in an old blanket. She unwrapped it and found a Bible, a worn and tattered copy of the Bible. It must have been Catherine's family Bible, she thought as she paged through it, seeing the family record pages. A slip of paper suddenly fell out and landed in her lap.

Madeline picked it up hopefully. It was the marriage lines. She had found them. Her father would be so proud!

Chapter Eleven

"This is going to be great fun," Anne assured Catherine.

"I never seen anything like it," Catherine said. Her eyes looked across the water toward the magic fairyland of lights and laughter as their boat skimmed across the river. The warm night air promised an evening of happiness, and with Simon at her side, how could that promise not be fulfilled? Her heart gladdened with excitement and she moved slightly closer to Simon as he took her hand.

"At home, public gardens were quite risqué," she told them. "Father never let me go there."

"I would not advise you to go to all of them here either," Mrs. Bradford said. "But Vauxhall usually has a more restrained crowd."

Their boat scraped against the wooden docking at the gate to the gardens, and a footman held it steady while another helped them all to alight. Lanterns lit a path through the trees ahead of them.

"Now, aren't you glad that you decided to come

along?" Nigel asked as he took Madeline's arm.

Madeline shrugged slightly. "It does not seem right somehow," she said, pulling her deep blue cloak more closely around her.

Catherine's heart lurched at even that vague reference to Edward, but somehow Simon knew. He took Catherine's arm with a reassuring squeeze as they followed the others along the lantern-lit path and through the gate.

"This is known as the Grand Walk," Simon told her as they entered a wide walkway.

"It seems fitting."

They were surrounded on both sides by stately trees, the branches curving gracefully overhead to form a natural colonnade to walk under. A footman came forward to lead them past several small temples and pavilions, and Catherine's breath slowed in wonder with each step she took. She'd never seen anything like this. It was all so splendid, so beautiful. Or maybe it was just the rush of happiness filling her heart lately. Maybe even the most mundane garden would seem magical with Simon at her side.

They passed a large rotunda off to their right, where an orchestra was playing so sweetly that her feet begged to dance, and then on past rows of supper boxes curving away to their left. The footman turned down the second row of boxes they came to and opened the door of the end box.

"Oh, this is a marvelous box," Anne said as she nudged Catherine. "I shall be able to see everyone who goes by."

"Is that important?" Catherine asked.

"Apparently to Anne it is." Simon laughed and sat down next to Catherine at the end of the box near the door.

While they waited for the footman to return with punch and sweets for nibbling, Catherine watched the people passing in fascination. The rainbow hues of their attire enchanted her.

"Would you like to dance?" Simon asked her.

"Oh, yes."

He led her out of the box and down the walks to the area set aside for dancing.

"You look particularly lovely tonight," Simon told her, pulling her arm a little more tightly through his. His eyes glowed with warmth as he gazed down at her soft yellow dress. "Too lovely to be wasted on this crowd. We should have stayed home."

"Oh, I am certain that you would find my company tiresome after a bit," she said with a teasing smile.

Simon laughed quietly. "You obviously underestimate yourself." She blushed under his steady regard which caused him to laugh even more. "I cannot imagine ever being bored in your company."

Catherine just smiled back, her joy too great to do anything but hug his words to her heart. Life was perfect. The orchestra began to play a waltz, and she moved comfortably into Simon's arms.

"Simon," she said after a moment. "When are

you going to tell your grandmother about Edward?"

Simon glanced down at her. "I haven't decided on a special time," he admitted. "When the time seems right, I will."

"Anne will be harder to tell," Catherine said.

"That is why I hope we can wait longer before telling anyone. Perhaps in a few weeks, or a month, she might be less emotional about his death," Simon said.

If the six months since Edward's death had not lessened Anne's grief, Catherine thought that one more month was not likely to erase it, but she did not say that to Simon. He knew the truth and still accepted her and Teddy, so it really did not matter that much when he told his family.

Madeline was rapidly regretting her decision to accompany the others to the gardens. Mrs. Bradford had persuaded her that she would do nothing improper for one in mourning; she did not have to dance or even stroll along the walks, just sit in the box and enjoy the evening air. But even sitting in the box seemed to be bordering on the disrespectful, Madeline feared.

"Good evening, Mrs. Bradford," a familiar voice called from the door to the box. "How ever did you manage to get everyone out of the house?"

"It was not easy, Michael," the older woman said with a laugh. "But I promised them we would be discreet."

202

Madeline frowned as her brother chuckled. She was not surprised to see him enjoying himself in a place such as this. He never really had appreciated Edward. A sudden thought wiped her frown away and made her turn to him, interrupting whatever nonsense he was saying to Anne and Nigel.

"Does Father happen to be here?" she asked eagerly.

"Yes, he is," Michael said. "He is in a box at the end of this walk. Prinny is expected to join him later."

"I did so want to speak to him," Madeline said apologetically to the others. "I hope you will excuse me." She got out of the box and took Michael's arm.

"I think I am expected to take her there," Michael said with mock surprise. He bowed slightly, then led his sister away.

"Really, Michael," Madeline snapped as soon as they were away from the box. "Must you make a joke out of everything? We are still in mourning, you know."

"I have not been allowed to forget," Michael noted. They walked a little farther, and Madeline saw her father up ahead. Two other gentlemen were in the box talking with him, but even as she and Michael approached, they stood up and left, leaving her father alone.

Lord Killian's eyes brightened when Madeline entered the box. "I was so hoping that I might see you here," he said.

Madeline glanced over at Michael, not feeling

able to speak freely in front of him. Surprisingly, he seemed to read her unspoken wish. "I think I shall take myself off," he said. "I am certain that Father will see you back to your box."

Lord Killian seemed barely to notice his son's departure. "Have you found anything?"

Madeline nodded, her excitement spilling over into her voice. "Yes, I found it yesterday. The very day you asked me to look."

"Yesterday!" Lord Killian seemed impressed. "Edward would be so proud of you."

Madeline's smile grew even wider with such praise. She put her reticule on the table and pulled out Catherine's marriage lines. After carefully unfolding them, she handed them across the table to her father and sat, waiting hopefully for his approval.

"This is marvelous, Madeline," her father said softly as he took the paper. He glanced at it briefly, to be certain it was indeed the right paper, then reached across the table and patted his daughter's hand. "You did a wonderful job."

His voice seemed disappointedly distracted though, and his hand stopped moving as he read the paper more carefully. She saw a slight frown crease his forehead.

Fear clutched at her heart. "Is something wrong with the paper?" she whispered in concern. "It is the right one, is it not?"

Lord Killian said nothing for a moment, but when he looked up, his eyes were bright with excitement. "Oh, yes, it is the right one," he nodded, carefully folding it. "Much better than I ever imagined," he added. Leaning forward slightly, he said, "Not only do I have the false marriage lines to use against our dear friend, but it seems that her father was none other than Patrick Dawes."

Madeline stared blankly at her father. Even though the name seemed to mean something to her father, she had never heard it before. "Is it that important?" she asked.

"Haven't you heard of him?" Lord Killian marveled, then shook his head. "Well, it does not matter." Leaning forward, he held the paper into the flame of the oil light.

Even as the flame leapt up to flick at the paper, Madeline felt fear flicking at her heart. "Ought we to destroy it?" she asked. "It looked so real. Are you certain—"

The anger in her father's glance quieted her. The quivering in her heart was now from fear she had displeased him.

"I just meant perhaps we needed proof of her treachery," she said quickly.

Lord Killian's eyes softened, but only slightly as the ashes of the paper fell onto the table. "If you need further proof that she is lying, there are Edward's letters. He told me himself that he hadn't married."

Madeline frowned. "He told you that? Why would he even think to mention such a thing?"

Her father waved away her questions. "Maybe the

205

trickster was after him even then. Who knows? Does it matter? We have that little lady right where we want her, and that's what is important. You know, I could not have done it without your help."

"I did it for Edward," Madeline said. But still her heart cried out with happiness at her father's words.

Anne had never considered Madeline among her favorite people, but she would be forever grateful to her for taking Michael away. Anne had thought she was bearing up quite well; most of the time she could laugh and talk and let Edward just hover unnoticed in the back of her mind. Except when Michael came around.

"Hello, again."

Anne's heart stopped as she saw Michael's smiling face.

"I thought that Anne might like to take a walk around the grounds with me," he suggested lightly.

Before Anne could protest, Mrs. Bradford spoke. "Why, how thoughtful of you," she cried. "I am certain Anne must be longing to leave this dreary box and join in the festivities."

But not with Michael! "Grandmother," Anne said with strained patience. "I am still in mourning."

Mrs. Bradford waved her hand at her granddaughter. "Walking in the gardens is not the same as dancing."

Michael opened the door to the box and stood waiting. Anne looked around her with exasperation, then, sighing loudly, she stood up and went out the door. "I should not be doing this," she told both Michael and her grandmother, but they only chuckled.

Michael offered Anne his arm, and once she had taken it, led her through the crowds.

"I do not know why you wanted to walk with me," Anne complained.

They reached the Grand Cross Walk, and Michael turned to his right. "Oh, I think you do," he said.

Anne glared at him, but the effect of it was lost because he wasn't even watching her. He was staring straight ahead with an annoying smile on his face. Fine, she could look away also, then. She needn't pay him any mind at all.

The strained silence lasted the whole time they walked along the Grand Cross Walk, and it began to be annoying. Why had he asked her to walk with him if he had nothing to say? Anne wondered crossly. If she had wanted silence, she could have stayed at home. A real gentleman would not go so long without making an attempt at conversation. But then, a real gentleman would not have forced her to walk with him when she so clearly hadn't wanted to.

They passed the South Walk and suddenly Anne noticed it was much darker and there were many fewer people about. She stopped walking, looking around her with a frown.

"Just where are we walking to?" she asked.

Michael held her hand onto his arm, and started

walking again. Anne allowed herself to be led along, but her footsteps dragged slightly as he turned off the main walkway onto a smaller, darker one.

"Michael."

"Actually we have a number of possibilities," Michael said lightly, as if he were unaware of Anne's growing anger. "We could turn to our right, go back slightly, and visit the ruins of Palmyra, or we can continue this way and choose between the Dark Walk, the Druid's Walk, or the Lover's Walk. Now, I myself would prefer the Lover's Walk, but—" He stopped suddenly as Anne pulled her hand away from him.

"Why are you doing this?" she hissed at him. Another couple passed them on the narrow walk, eyeing them curiously, and Anne tried to keep her voice low. "Is this some sort of joke?"

Michael sighed in exasperation and took her arm, more roughly this time, pulling her along the path until he spotted a bench under some trees. He hurried over to it, slowing only when she stumbled slightly on the rough ground off the path. When they reached the stone bench, Michael took hold of her upper arms tightly, and forced her to sit next to him.

"A joke?" he cried, his voice raw with sudden emotion. "I do not see anything even remotely funny about the hell you are putting both of us through."

Anne pulled sharply away from him. "It is your

own fault if you are upset about something," she informed him coldly. "You don't have to be here in town. You could have stayed in the country, or gone to Bath, or anyplace else. You did not have to come to Grandmother's party, or to Vauxhall tonight. You know how I feel, and you should just stay away." Her voice lost its strength as she spoke and tears quivered along with the last of her words.

"But I cannot stay away, Anne." Michael's voice had lost its anger and had become soft and pleading. "And it is because I do know how you feel." His hands reached out for her again, pulling her close to him. "Oh, Anne," he sighed as his lips bent down to meet hers.

For a moment Anne clung to him and kissed him back with the same desperate intensity with which he was kissing her. It had been so long and she had missed him so much. Her arms, her heart, had never felt so empty as they had these last few months. His arms tightened around her, his lips vowed to her heart that he would never let her go. For a moment her heart sang with joy, but then memories flooded her soul and the song died out. Her lips left his and she drew back from him. He didn't try to stop her.

"Oh, Michael, why did you have to do that?" Anne said brokenly. She turned away from him, her head bent. "What does it change?"

Michael reached over to pick up her right hand. "Anne, when are you going to stop this farce? We have done nothing wrong. Why are you so intent on making us suffer?"

"Michael, please, you do not understand," she said, her voice unsteady with pain and tears.

"You are right," he snapped, and dropped her hand. "I do not understand. You loved me before Edward died. Now, when you are free, I am not to come near you."

"We have been all through this before." Anne sighed and wearily rose to her feet. "I see no point in discussing it again."

But Michael wasn't so easily dismissed. He grabbed her hand and pulled her back down the bench. "I see no point in this whole masquerade we have been living, but I was willing to give you time." He said nothing for a moment, and then, when he spoke again, his voice reflected uncertainty. "You said that you did not love Edward."

"No, no, I did not," Anne said quickly in a rush to reassure him. When Michael did not respond, she squeezed his hand gently. "I accepted him only because I thought we were reasonably well matched and there were no other suitors waiting in line."

"Then for heaven's sake, mourn him and be done with it," Michael cried. "And let us get on with our lives. Stop shutting me out as if we mean nothing to each other, and as if your heart is locked away in some grave in Canada."

Anne put her hands up to her face and tried to wipe her tears away, but the pain came in sudden jolts that she wasn't strong enough to face. "I cannot," she said, her words broken with sobs and her tears flowing down over her hands. Michael pulled her close and let her lay against his chest as she cried.

"If only I had never written him that letter," she said. "If only I had not wanted to be free before he returned, I would know that my news had nothing to do with his death, and we could be together. But I do not know." She pulled slightly back from him and stared up into Michael's unhappy face. "What if he loved me and could not bear the thought of us being married? We might have killed him."

Michael's hands touched her gently, rubbing the back of her neck as he tried to ease some of her suffering. "Edward was not like that," he told her. "And there was no hint that there was anything strange in the letter from his commanding officer about his death." But they both knew that the vaguely worded letter actually said very little.

Anne stayed in the blissful security of Michael's arms for a few moments longer. Her heart was too weak to deprive her of such little snatches of happiness, but her pain was too great to enjoy the moment as she wanted. She reluctantly pulled away from him.

"We had better go back," she said.

He nodded and rose to his feet, helping her up also. "This is not the end of it."

His words held a gentle warning and a promise of hope, but she just shook her head. "Forget about me, Michael. Find someone else."

Michael took her arm and led her back to the

walkway. "I love you, and I know you love me," he said firmly. "Sooner or later, you will forget this nonsense and be willing to marry me. I can wait."

Anne sighed, and they walked back to her grandmother's box in silence. Michael left her there, which was what she wanted, she told herself, for his presence was just too disturbing. But it was not easy, sitting with her grandmother and watching Simon and Catherine. It was obvious, in every move they made, that they cared about each other. Anne felt even more alone, knowing that she would never have that kind of happiness.

She even felt jealous of Nigel and Madeline, and they were not a loving couple by any means. But they did belong to each other, and that was a feeling that Anne would never know.

Chapter Twelve

"I am afraid that I shall be occupied all morning," Simon apologized one morning about a week after their trip to Vauxhall. "My lawyers need me to sign some papers they have drawn up, and then we need to go over some further business. I may not even be finished by lunchtime."

"You must not worry about me," Catherine protested. She sipped the rest of her tea and pushed the cup away from her. "I have a number of little chores I have neglected shamefully that will keep me busy all day."

"So I will not be missed, is that it?" Simon laughed as he stood up.

"I did not say that," Catherine quickly assured him.

Simon laughed again. They were alone in the dining room and he walked over to her chair, leaning down to kiss her lightly on the lips. "Behave yourself while I am gone," he teased.

Catherine made a face at him, but feared her love

was shining through too much to give it the fierce effect she had hoped for and laughed instead. Her heart seemed overflowing with happiness. She hadn't thought that life could hold so much joy. Once Simon had left, she stood up also and wandered up to the nursery to check on Teddy, but he was more than content with Bessie, so there was little for Catherine to do for him. How lucky the two of them were! she thought. Because of Simon's kindness, they had a secure home and people who cared about them.

Catherine smiled as she came back down the stairs. It was funny, she thought. The husband she had thought she loved she had barely been able to live with, while the one she married for convenience was the one she truly loved.

As she reached the foyer outside the sitting room, a footman brought a piece of paper over to her. "This came fer you, madam," he said.

Catherine took the note from him and looked at it in bewilderment, not recognizing the handwriting or the seal that closed the back. After thanking the footman, she took it into the deserted sitting room, closing the door softly behind her.

Catherine walked across the room to sit in the sun on the wide window seat. Once she was settled, she ripped open the note and immediately glanced at the signature. It was from Lord Killian and her heart jolted to a stop.

The note was very short and direct. "Meet me at the north end of the rose garden in Hyde Park at 11 a.m. Lord Killian."

If that was not like him, Catherine thought angrily. All he had to do was issue an order and she was supposed to jump and obey. It would be a pleasure to show him that she was not afraid of him.

Crumpling up the paper, Catherine tossed it into the cold fireplace and took her sewing basket from the corner. She had started embroidering some handkerchiefs for Mrs. Bradford a few days before, and for several minutes sewed with determination. Then she suddenly threw down the stitchery and went to pick up the note. She smoothed it out and reread the words. Perhaps she ought to see what he wanted, she thought, her hands trembling slightly. After all, she did not have anything very pressing to do this morning. She did not admit fear to herself, but knew it was there. What would he do to her if she did not go? If only Simon were here to consult.

Once she made up her mind to go, it did not take her long to get ready. She put on a bright yellow straw bonnet that matched her yellow walking dress and put a light shawl over her shoulders, hoping the cheery colors would lend her courage. She was glad that neither Anne nor Mrs. Bradford was around, for she did not want to make any explanations. A footman was the only one who saw her leave the house as the clock in the hallway chimed eleven.

Catherine hurried the few blocks to Hyde Park, knowing that she was going to be late and telling herself that it hardly mattered. She was not his servant to be at his beck and call. For all he knew, she hadn't been at home when the note had been delivered. Once she reached the rose garden, she saw

Lord Killian striding impatiently about and hid a smile. She purposely kept her steps slow and steady as she approached him.

"You are late," he snapped as he pulled a watch from his vest pocket and glanced at the time.

She chose not to defend herself. "What did you want to see me about?"

Lord Killian glanced around the garden. When he saw no one else there, he pulled a paper from an inside coat pocket. "I want you to sign this," he told her.

Catherine frowned as she took the paper from him. "What is this?" she asked.

Lord Killian shrugged. "It is merely an agreement that you will make no claim on Edward's estate."

"I have already told you that I want nothing from his estate," she pointed out, then, unfolding the paper, she began to read. She didn't have to go any farther than the first few lines to realize that in signing this paper, she would be saying that she and Edward had never been married, and that Teddy was illegitimate and not entitled to any part of Edward's estate.

"I would never sign something like this," she cried angrily, and pushed the paper back into his hands.

"I think you had better," he said.

"And just how do you plan to force me?"

"If you do not sign this paper, I shall feel it is my duty to tell Simon and his family that you are Patrick Dawes's daughter."

Catherine just stared at him. "So?"

"So perhaps you are not aware of your father's

varied career before he fled the country."

Catherine glanced beyond him for a moment. The bright sunlight danced over the lawn, the roses lending a delicate scent to the air that soothed the worry in her heart. "What are you talking about?"

Lord Killian's smile was unpleasant. "Merely that you father often helped people invest their money. Unfortunately, it was discovered after he left that the money people had given him had merely helped to finance his flight."

"Are you saying my father was a thief?" she asked carefully, her voice held in tight control.

Lord Killian ignored her question. "The last of his investors was James Bradford."

Simon's father! Catherine's heart sank and her bravado faltered.

"He was perhaps the most naive, as well as the last," Lord Killian went on. "For he was not content with investing a few thousand pounds like most of the others, but entrusted his whole fortune to your father."

Catherine folded her arms in front of her body, her hands tightly clutching her elbows in an attempt to keep the horror rising within her from showing on her face. Her father had cheated Simon's family out of their money?

"Unfortunately," Lord Killian went on smoothly, as if he were aware of her struggle and found it amusing, "Bradford could not weather such a loss and saw only one way out of the scandal and disgrace he had gotten himself into. He killed himself."

Catherine's stomach lurched in protest. She knew that all the blood had left her face, and bit her bottom lip to keep from crying out. She could deny Lord Killian's words, but what point would there be in that? She had learned too much about her father since his death to disbelieve what had been said, but that didn't stop the shame from filling her soul.

"The paper?" Lord Killian repeated.

Catherine blinked quickly and saw that Lord Killian was holding the paper out to her once more.

"There is an inn across from the park where you can sign it," he said pleasantly as if they were discussing the weather.

She took a step back and looked up at him with a frown. "I told you I was not signing that. I have not changed my mind."

Lord Killian could not believe his ears. "Have you any idea what will happen once people learn who your father was?" he snapped. "You will not be welcomed anywhere, possibly not even by your husband and his family."

"Oh, come now," she said, trying to sound braver than she felt. "All that happened twenty years ago, and I was not involved."

"No, but there are enough people still about who remember your father with hatred and would like nothing better than to revenge their loss on you," he pointed out.

"And is that not the very thing that you are doing?" Catherine lost all patience with him. She wasn't sure where her sudden strength came from, but it was there to hold her fast to the way that was right and fair.

"Are you not trying to make me pay for your son's death? Well, I am tired of your threats. They do not frighten me at all! I shall not sign your monstrous paper!" She grabbed it from his hand and while he stared at her in astonishment, she ripped it to pieces and flung them to the ground. "I was married to your son, and all your denials will never change that fact."

"You are a fool," Lord Killian shouted.

She shrugged and turned away, striding angrily down the path.

"I shall tell everyone," he called after her. "Do not think my kind heart will change my mind."

Catherine did not even look back at him. She walked out of the park and down the few streets to her home, too upset to notice anything around her.

How dare that man try to threaten her into giving up what was rightfully Teddy's! Did he truly think that just because her father had behaved despicably in the past that she would act that way also? Did he believe she would be willing to cheat her own son? How she hated that man!

Catherine had never been so angry before in her entire life and she was determined to fight him. She would make him sorry that he ever dared to cross her. And if he actually did tell about her father, well, she might be disgraced but she would make certain that Lord Killian was also.

Her footsteps slowed slightly as she thought about her father. There was no doubt in her mind that he had done the things Lord Killian had accused him of, but she wondered how many people would remember him. Of course, Simon and his family would, and that was all that would really matter to her.

Some of Catherine's anger faded away as sadness took its place. Was it only this morning that she had been so happy with her life? Was she now facing the prospect of losing all that because of Lord Killian's vindictiveness?

A footman let Catherine into the house and she nodded to him absently as she tried to decide what to do. She was not going to sit back quietly and wait for Lord Killian to make his move to destroy her. There had to be a way to fight him. She walked slowly up to her room, stopping just inside the bedroom door to scold herself. Why was she being so mollycoddled? She had the perfect means to fight him. All she had to do was take her marriage lines to a lawyer.

She tossed her bonnet onto the dressing table, her shawl down next to it. Grabbing a branch of candles from the desk, she left her room and hurried up the stairs to the attic. She found her trunk with no trouble, but when she pushed open the top, she was puzzled by the disarray she found. She thought she had packed things more neatly than that. But she pushed her confusion aside and found the package that held her Bible and flipped through the pages. The lines weren't there.

She frowned and began to page through the book more slowly, but there still was no sign of the paper. Maybe it had fallen out, she thought, and searched through the trunk. Nothing. She sat back on her heels and stared ahead of her in worried confusion.

She was certain she had put the lines into the Bible, so why weren't they there now? It was not as if they were something terribly valuable that someone might steal.

Blast! she whispered, trembling slightly with sudden fear, as if cold wind had blown through her heart. How stupid she had been! Of course they were valuable—they were all the proof she had that she and Edward had truly married, and that Teddy was his heir. They were the only way she could fight Lord Killian and his hatred, and now they were gone. Lord Killian had her trapped.

Catherine walked back to her bedroom in a daze. She could not believe she had been so stupid as to think she could win against Lord Killian. She was nothing but a silly naive child alongside him.

After closing the door quietly, Catherine walked across her room and sank down on her bed. She was certainly in trouble now. Not only had she refused to sign Lord Killian's paper, but she had fought with him and made him angry so that he would be sure to do everything he could to ruin her. And there was not one single thing she could do to stop him.

She covered her face with her hands as she thought of Simon's reaction to the news about her father. He had been understanding about Edward, but then, he had not really been involved in that, nor was there anything shameful about it. This was far different. Her father's dishonesty had caused his father's death. There was no way that he could be understanding about that.

Catherine sighed and rose to her feet. She wandered aimlessly around the room, thinking how the people she cared about would be hurt. She knew that society was rarely fair. After her father's death revealed his unscrupulous dealings in Halifax, hadn't she been punished for his misdeeds? The same would happen here except that she would not be the only one punished. Mrs. Bradford and Anne might also be ostracized.

Of course, that was assuming that she remained a part of their family. There was always the possibility that Simon would have their marriage annulled or would divorce her when he learned the truth. But either of those actions would also bring some measure of disgrace to the family. It didn't seem fair that anyone else should have to suffer.

Catherine stopped and stared out the window. Maybe there was a way to save them from scandal. Maybe there was a way to keep Lord Killian's revelations from having any power.

She turned around. "If I were not here," she murmured, "it would make no difference what he told everyone. His words can hurt Simon's family only if I am part of it. If I am gone, it will all pass over quickly." And save Simon the embarrassment of having to send her away.

As soon as Catherine said the words, she knew that this was the only thing she could do. She would leave, quietly and without any fuss, taking Teddy with her. Just where she would go was a problem though. For Simon's sake, it ought to be far from London and London society. And then there was the question of how she and Teddy would live. If only she had some relatives that she could go to for help.

Of course, she cried to herself, that would be the perfect solution. She would go to her relatives—her mother's family in Boston. She would be far from Simon and his family, yet would not be left to fend for herself. All she needed was enough money for passage.

Simon had given her an ample allowance just a few weeks before and she had spent very little of it. She hurried over to her dressing table and pulling out the little wooden chest that held her money. She counted it carefully. With luck it should be enough. The trick would be finding passage to Boston. With the war still on, she was going to have to sail to a neutral port first. It was bound to cost more.

Well, she would just have to be very frugal, she decided firmly as she looked around her. Most of her traveling things were packed in her trunk, so the first step was to go back to the attic. She picked up the candles and trudged back up the stairs.

She could not pack a whole trunkload of things to take along. It would be far too hard to manage on her own, plus make it very difficult to slip out of the house. Luckily, she found a sturdy bag made of carpet in a corner of the attic. It was slightly shabby but would serve her needs well. She stuffed her Bible into it along with an old shawl that had been her mother's and some family jewelry that was of more sentimental value than monetary. Then she hurried back down the stairs.

Once in her own room, she packed another dress, a change of undergarments for herself, and a heavy cloak that Simon had insisted that she buy. Next she would have to get Teddy's things. She closed the bag and put it in the bottom of her wardrobe. Then she smoothed down her hair, took a deep breath, and went down the hall to the nursery.

Teddy was asleep and Bessie was knitting quietly near the window. She looked up with a smile as Catherine came in the room.

"How is he?" Catherine asked.

Bessie smiled toward the cradle. "Oh, he's as good as gold, that little laddie is."

Catherine looked down at her son, then up at Bessie. "I would like to sit with him awhile, so if you have something else to do . . ."

"Well, I could check on that fool girl. She was to bring clean linens up 'ere a whiles ago," Bessie said. She rose heavily to her feet and walked across the room. "I'll be back right quick," she added from the door.

"Take your time," Catherine called. "I may even take him for a walk. It is so lovely out."

Bessie looked slightly surprised and slightly disapproving. "If you wish, ma'am."

"I do," Catherine said, forcing her voice to be colder than normal and more dismissing.

Bessie nodded and left the room. As soon as the door closed, Catherine hurried over to Teddy's dressing table and picked out an assortment of clothes for him. It was going to be hard to squeeze them all into the bag, but she would need them.

She went to the door and opened it slowly, looking down the hall before she went out. No one was in sight, so she slipped out the door and back to her own room. There she stuffed Teddy's things into the bag and put it back on the wardrobe floor.

The only thing left, besides the actual leaving, was to write the note to Simon, and that would be the hardest thing she had to do. There was so much she'd like to say to him and so little time. Slowly, she picked up some paper, a pen, and the bottle of ink from the desk in her room and walked back to the nursery.

There was a small table in one corner of Teddy's room, and she settled herself at it to write. It was hard to find the right words, but after three attempts she was satisfied, not happy with it, but satisfied it was the best she could do. Putting her pen down, she reread the letter.

Dear Simon,

Today I have learned of my father's, Patrick Dawes's, involvement with your father. You were very understanding about Edward, but I know that this is far different. Hopefully by leaving I can save you and your family from any hint of scandal. I want you to know I shall always remember your many kindnesses to me.

Catherine

With a sigh Catherine folded it carefully and, carrying it and the writing tools, went back to her room. She wrote Simon's name on the outside of the paper and left it on the desk. After taking a last look around at the room that had become so beloved to her, she pulled the bag from the wardrobe. She took her money from the little wooden chest and wrapped most of it in a small blanket of Teddy's, then put it in the bag. The rest of the money went into her reticule.

Hurrying back to the nursery, Catherine got Teddy and wrapped him in a light blanket. She brought him to her room and laid him on the bed while she put on her bonnet and shawl. Then she picked up Teddy, her bag, and her reticule.

"Good-bye, Simon," she whispered to the silence, then hurried out into the hall.

No one was around as she went quietly down the stairs. Below, a footman answered the front door and showed someone into the sitting room, but by the time she reached the foyer, no one was in sight. Now was the time for whispered good-byes, but she hadn't the strength. Brushing a quick tear from her eye, she let herself out the front door quickly and hurried away down the street.

"I think it is marvelous that you are getting out more." Mrs. Bradford stopped her knitting to smile at Anne. "Why don't you invite Michael to come in with you after your drive. It should be just about time for tea by then."

Anne glanced at her grandmother, not overly excited about the prospect of spending even more time with Michael. "I doubt that he will have time. He's leaving town tomorrow, you know."

"Is he? What a shame. I'll miss him. He's such a pleasant young man," her grandmother went on.

Anne glanced at her wryly, then walked over to the window to look out. "I shall not be sorry to see him go." Her reflection stared back in mockery.

Her grandmother shook her head and started her knitting again. "You may not be, but I imagine there are several other women in London who will be."

Anne turned around quickly, fear leaping into her heart. "What are you talking about?"

Mrs. Bradford shrugged her shoulders innocently. "Just that now that he is the heir to that estate he has become quite eligible. I know of at least three mothers who are hoping for a match between him and their daughter."

"That is ridiculous," Anne cried, and walked back to sit near her grandmother.

"Is it? What is strange about a young man marrying? Most men do, you know," Mrs. Bradford said calmly. She was concentrating on her knitting and missed Anne's frown.

They heard a knock at the door and a few minutes later a footman brought Michael to the sitting room.

"Ah, Michael." Mrs. Bradford looked up as he entered. "I hear you are leaving us. We shall miss you."

Michael smiled at her, then glanced over at Anne, who just stared coldly back at him. "I am flattered to hear that my absence will be noticed," he said.

"Shall we go?" Anne asked. "I want to be back here before tea."

Mrs. Bradford shook her head. "You must not mind her, Michael. She has been in bad spirits all day."

"Perhaps she is sorry to see me leave," he suggested lightly.

"Yes, that must be it," Mrs. Bradford agreed.

Anne frowned at them both as she walked toward the door. After nodding to Mrs. Bradford, Michael followed her. He determinedly placed her hand upon his arm and led her out to his carriage. Her heart raced at his nearness in spite of her orders for it to behave.

"You could at least smile once or twice," Michael commented as he handed her up into the curricle. "Tomorrow your wish will come true and I will be gone."

"Then tomorrow I will smile," she said, looking straight ahead of her.

Michael sighed and climbed up into the carriage himself. "If you feel that way, why did you bother to come out with me?" he asked as he let the horses move into the middle of the road.

Anne shrugged her shoulders, her eyes still focused on some distant point. "Because you are leaving," she said in a tight little voice.

"Oh, Anne, why must we always play this little game?" he asked as he rounded a corner.

His question really expected no answer, and Anne had none for him. No new answer, that is. They'd been down every path of this argument before, trod every inch of it and found no answers. Maybe there were none to be found. None except staying apart. She kept her head turned as if fascinated by the houses they passed, and Michael drove in silence.

"Grandmother thinks that you will marry soon," she said after a while, finally gaining the courage to look at him.

Michael turned to see her eyes. "Does that thought upset you?"

It wasn't the answer she expected, or the one she wanted to hear. Her courage deserted her and she turned her gaze away. "I am certain that you will want an heir, especially now that you will inherit the estate and the title," she admitted. Her voice was quite calm.

"I am so glad that you understand," he said cynically. "I just hope that you approve of my choice."

Anne spun back quickly to face him. The blood had drained from her face; the world grew blurry and danced before her eyes. "You have already chosen someone?"

Michael sighed. "You know that I intend to marry you."

"Oh." The receding of her fears accompanied such a rush of relief that Anne felt weak. She bent her head to stare down at her hands. "I thought you meant someone else."

"It would be what you deserve if I did marry some other girl," he said.

229

Anne just nodded but kept her eyes down, fighting back tears. It was a losing battle.

"Blast!" Michael muttered after a telltale sniff. "What the devil are you crying for? You're the one that keeps refusing to marry me."

Anne took a handkerchief from her reticule and tried to stop the tears, but in just a moment she was sobbing into a soggy piece of embroidered linen.

Why was her heart so foolish? If Michael was not to be part of her future, then she had to let him go. She had to stop living for his smile and waiting for his touch. She had to be strong enough to go on with her life alone.

The carriage stopped moving, and Anne looked up. They were in the yard of the Royal George Inn. Before Anne could say a word, Michael had jumped down and was around to her side of the curricle, helping her out. A stable boy was holding the horses' heads.

"Take them around to the stables," Michael told him, and keeping a firm grip on Anne's arm, led her inside the inn.

"What are we doing here?" Anne asked through her tears.

"I can hardly drive through the streets of London with you sobbing at my side," he told her as he led her inside. The innkeeper was down a hall to their right, approaching the door to a private parlor, so Michael led her down that way. Before they could reach the man, the innkeeper pushed open the door and leaned inside.

"The coach for Southampton is out front," he announced.

"Sir!" Michael called to the man. "Sir, could you—"

But even as he spoke, a young woman came out of the parlor next to the innkeeper, struggling to hold a baby and carry a bag at the same time. Anne and Michael both froze.

"Catherine?" Anne cried.

Simon returned home in the middle of the afternoon, not as early as he would have liked, but in time to have tea with Catherine and plan their evening together, a prospect that was infinitely appealing. Except that she seemed to be nowhere around. He walked into the sitting room, where Nigel and his grandmother were seated.

"Where is Catherine?" Simon asked. Her sewing basket was there on the window seat.

"I thought she was upstairs," Mrs. Bradford said.

"No, I was just up there, changing for tea, and did not see her," Simon said. "It's not like her to go off without telling anyone. Did she tell you at lunch if she was going out?"

Mrs. Bradford shook her head. "No, I wasn't down for lunch. I had a bad headache and ate in my room. I came down just a short time ago, when Anne was going out with Michael."

"Have you looked in the nursery?" Nigel asked.

"Yes, but she wasn't there either." Simon picked up her sewing as if it could give him some clue to her whereabouts. A nagging cloud of worry had cast a shadow across his heart. "Teddy was gone too," he told them.

Mrs. Bradford stood up with a laugh. "There you are, then. She must be somewhere in the house. She's not likely to take Teddy out shopping with her." She pulled the bell pull in the corner, and a moment later a footman came to the door. "Ask the young Mrs. Bradford to come here," she said to him. He nodded and left.

"You must not worry so, Simon," his grandmother scolded gently as she walked back to her chair. "I know you are very fond of Catherine, but she is not likely to disappear the moment you take your eyes off her."

Simon nodded and tossed the sewing back onto the window seat before coming to sit near his grandmother. "I guess I am being a bit silly," he said with a grin. "I still cannot quite believe how lucky I am to have found her."

A quiet knock announced the return of the footman, but he was alone. "Bessie said the young Mrs. Bradford went out, ma'am," he said.

"Went out?" Simon was on his feet in an instant, that cloud of worry now a full-fledged storm. "Where is Teddy?"

The footman stared blankly at him.

"For God's sake, get Bessie, will you?" Simon snapped. The footman nodded and hurried out.

Bessie was more specific. "She took Master Teddy and went out. Just before lunch."

"Before lunch?" Simon cried, and ran his fingers

through his hair. What was going on? Were his fears justified, or was he letting his imagination run wild? "Did my wife say where she was going?"

But Bessie had told all she knew.

"That will be all, thank you." Mrs. Bradford dismissed Bessie, then came to take Simon's hand, pulling him back down on the sofa.

"Obviously, you fear something is wrong," she said to Simon. "What do you think happened?"

Simon just shrugged, forcing a brave smile to hide his fears. "It's just that I don't understand where she would have gone." He hated being still. His feet were restless and wanted to pace, but he knew that sign of anxiety would only worry his grandmother more. After all, there was no reason to suspect that there was something wrong. "It is not like her to leave without telling someone where she was going?"

No reason? Simon thought suddenly of Lord Killian. Could he be behind this?

"Perhaps she did," Mrs. Bradford pointed out. "Maybe she left a message with one of the servants we haven't questioned or maybe she left you a note. Did you check your room?"

Simon shook his head. "No, I didn't think to."

"Then why not look now?" his grandmother suggested.

Simon hurried up to their room. There was no note on her dressing table or in his dressing room. The little table near the bed, the washstand, and the mantel were all empty. He was about to leave the room when he passed the desk and saw the note

233

lying there.

For some reason his heart seemed to stop. He picked it up almost fearfully and unfolded it. He read it once. Then he read it again. But it made no sense. All that he could understand was that she felt she had to leave for some reason. Clutching it in his hand, he hurried down to the sitting room.

"She is gone," he told his grandmother and Nigel.

"Gone? Why? Where?" Mrs. Bradford nodded toward the note in his hand. "Does she give you any reasons?"

Simon shook his head, then read the note to them. "It doesn't make any sense to me. Who the devil is Patrick Dawes?"

Mrs. Bradford waved the question aside as if it were of no consequence. "Oh, he is just a Captain Sharp who tricked your father out of some money. But what was that about Edward in the letter?"

Simon stared down at the letter in his hand. He had barely noticed the reference himself, having dismissed Edward long ago as unimportant to their lives, yet there it was. This was hardly the time he would have chosen to tell his grandmother the truth about Catherine and Edward but, like it or not, he would have to.

He sat down heavily, not certain where to begin. He glanced up and found Nigel's gaze on him. Simon remembered Nigel and Madeline's mockery that first day back, and how he'd felt pushed into those rash statements that his grandmother had misinterpreted. Then he thought of Catherine and how complete his life had been these last few weeks with her at his side. The past was of little import beside the present and the future, their future together.

"Things were not always as they seemed," he began slowly. "You see, Catherine was a widow when I met her. A widow with a son."

Nigel whistled softly in surprise, but Mrs. Bradford's face fell. "Then Teddy is not your son?" she asked.

Simon shook his head slowly. "There seemed to be no way to tell you without telling it all, and Anne was so upset, I thought it best to wait."

"Anne?" Nigel repeated. "What does she have to do with this?"

Simon leaned back so he could see both his grandmother and Nigel at once. "Catherine had been married to Edward. She was his widow."

"Oh, my Lord," Mrs. Bradford said with a deep sigh. "Poor Anne. How that will hurt."

"Will it?" Nigel asked. "I never thought she truly could have loved Edward. Not the Anne we grew up with."

"I wouldn't have thought so either, but the tears . . ." Mrs. Bradford said. "She seems truly distraught."

Simon got to his feet. "Maybe we were wrong to try to protect her. Maybe knowing the truth about Edward will stop this determination she has to mourn him all her life. Catherine could certainly tell her that he was not a saint." Simon pounded the back of the sofa. "Once we get Catherine back here where she belongs, that is."

"Do you have any idea where she might have

gone, Simon?" Mrs. Bradford asked him quietly.

He shook his head, trying to also shake off his despair. "She has no one in this country but us. Lord Killian refused to recognize her or Teddy when she first came here."

"Why, that scoundrel!" Mrs. Bradford cried.

"Scoundrel, indeed. And I'll wager he's involved in this in some way."

"She cannot be very far away if she left only a few hours ago," Nigel pointed out. "Did she have enough money to hire a coach?"

Simon nodded. "So she could be out of the city by now," he said. "I think it's time to pay Teddy's grandfather a visit. If for no other reason than to have the pleasure of throttling him."

"Sounds like a visit to be remembered," Nigel said with a sudden grin. "Mind if I come along?"

Chapter Thirteen

Catherine looked from Anne's astonished face to Michael's, then Teddy began to cry. What terrible luck she was having, she thought as she frantically tried to quiet the baby. She heard the commotion from the inn yard as passengers disembarked from the coach.

"The coach won't stop for mor'n a minute," the innkeeper warned, and went off to greet the new arrivals.

"Catherine, what are you doing here?" Anne asked, then peered around her into the parlor. "Where is Simon?"

"He's not here," Catherine said after a moment's hesitation. Through the open inn door beyond Michael and Anne she saw people boarding the coach. "I really can't stop now," she apologized with a quick smile she hoped would allay their obvious suspicions. "Simon will explain all this when you see him."

Michael moved slightly, blocking her way so she couldn't get past him. "Why are you going to Southampton?"

Only two passengers were left standing, waiting to board. "I don't have time to talk," she argued. "I really have to—"

"Oh, Catherine, you are not leaving Simon, are you?" Anne cried suddenly, and grabbed ahold of her hand. The bag fell to the floor and some of Teddy's things spilled out. "You cannot do that. We all love you."

How had Anne jumped to that conclusion? Catherine wondered. Were her intentions so transparent? She grabbed up the bag, clumsily stuffing the clothes back into it. "You do not know anything about me," she pointed out sharply. Over Michael's shoulder she saw the driver of the coach helping an old woman into it. If she was going to make the coach, she had to get away now. There was no more time for niceties. She turned to Anne, her heart cold as ice.

"How would you feel if you knew that I had been married to Edward?" Catherine cried. "That the fiancé you're mourning so had found someone else? That I had his son instead of you."

Anne looked as shocked as Catherine had expected, but not angry or repulsed. "You were married to Edward?" she whispered.

"Yes," Catherine said coldly. "Now do you want me to stay here? Or will you let me get on my coach and leave?"

238

Michael took the bag from her hand and for a moment of blessed relief Catherine thought he was going to carry it to the coach for her, but he tossed it back into the parlor. Hadn't they heard her confession? Weren't they angry with her?

"I have to go," she argued, close to tears.

"Yes," Michael said calmly. "You have to go back into the parlor and explain yourself."

"But that is the last coach for Southampton today," Catherine told him. What good would it do to tell the whole ugly story? It would just delay her departure for a day and cost her room and board at the inn.

But Michael was not to be denied. He took her arm with one hand and put his other arm around Anne's shoulders, leading them both into the parlor. Through the open doorway at the end of the hall, Catherine saw the driver climb up onto the coach. A moment later she heard it drive away from the inn. Her heart sank as Michael closed the door.

Catherine walked slowly over to a wooden settee in the middle of the room and sat down. Teddy was still fussing slightly, and she absently tried to quiet him. Anne came to sit next to her.

"Was it true?" she whispered to Catherine. "Were you really married to Edward?"

Catherine nodded, suddenly too weary to speak. Why had she thought she could protect anyone? She could barely take care of herself and Teddy.

"And did he marry you while he was engaged to me?" Anne continued.

Catherine nodded again, then turned to look at Anne with tear-filled eyes. "I didn't want to hurt you," she said weakly. The tears began to run silently down her cheeks.

Without a word Anne took Teddy from Catherine's unresisting arms and carried him across the floor to Michael. "Hold him, will you?" Anne ordered more than asked, and put the baby into his arms. Michael stared at Teddy in dismay as the baby stared back with equal uncertainty.

Anne returned to her place next to Catherine, putting her arms around her. "You mustn't cry," Anne scolded gently.

"When I came I had no idea that Edward had been engaged to anyone else, certainly not to Simon's sister," Catherine explained, tears streaming down her cheeks. "I never wanted to hurt you."

"You didn't hurt me," Anne said, but Catherine knew she was just saying that. How could Anne not be hurt by hearing about Edward? She had loved him. Finally Catherine's tears slowed and she sat up.

"I'm sorry," Catherine whispered.

She saw Anne and Michael exchange glances, then Anne turned back to Catherine. "Can you tell us how he died?" she asked quietly.

Catherine looked puzzled. "Weren't you told?" She looked from Anne to Michael and, realizing that he was still holding Teddy, went to take the baby from him. "Are you sure it will not upset you further? You have been very kind about our marriage, but I know how you loved him. . . ."

"No," Anne said quickly. "I did not love him. We were to marry for convenience. There was no stronger feeling on either side. At least," she added hesitantly, "I do not think there was."

Catherine just shook her head in confusion, then brought Teddy back to the bench. Anne had to have loved Edward. Why else would she have been so upset? "Edward was killed in a tavern fight," Catherine told them.

Michael moved a chair closer to the two women and sat down. "But what was the fight about? How did it start?"

Catherine frowned. "What does all this matter?"

Michael and Anne exchanged glances, then he reached out his hand and Anne took it as Catherine watched in amazement. "You love Michael, not Edward!" she cried, relief washing over her heart.

Anne nodded. "But I was engaged to Edward. When we discovered how we felt, I wrote him. He must have just gotten the letter before he died, and we have been afraid . . . well, that it upset him and somehow caused his death."

Catherine's relief and joy subsided slightly. "I have no idea if he got the letter," she had to admit.

Anne bit her bottom lip and shrugged. "It was silly to think you would know."

The sorrow on Anne's face was more than Catherine could bear. "But I did know Edward," she went on. Looking at the two of them, she took a deep breath. "After we were married, Edward had

241

other women. Maybe it was partly my fault. I was very young and did not know much about men. He made no secret of his liaisons and used to taunt me with them."

She glanced away, blinking back the tears that the memories had awoken. Tears of pain and humiliation, not a broken heart. "The night Edward was killed, he had gone to his current mistress and discovered her with another man. Edward was drunk, tried to fight him, and lost. I do not think your letter could have been to blame for his death."

No one said a word for a long moment. Even the hustle and bustle of the inn seemed to have died away into silence. Then Michael coughed in embarrassment. "I don't know how to apologize for my brother's actions," he said. "I would never have guessed that he would act like such a swine."

Catherine gave him a tight smile. No, Michael would not expect a man would act that way. He would make Anne a wonderful husband. Catherine only wished she'd be around to see them happy together. "Well, does that answer your questions?" she asked, rising to her feet briskly. Lingering over wistfulness would not help her now. Perhaps there were other ways of getting to Southampton. The mail coach perhaps.

Anne let go of Michael's hand to hug Catherine. "Yes, it does, and thank you."

Catherine kept her smile in place and stepped around the end of the bench. Her bag was on the floor near the door. The innkeeper should know how she could leave London.

"Actually, it does not answer all of them," Michael noted.

Catherine stopped to stare at him.

"You never did explain what you are doing here," he reminded her.

She looked uneasy. "I am going back to Boston," she said.

"But why?" Anne cried. "If it is because of Edward . . ."

"No, it is not," Catherine said, dread filling her heart again. "It is because of my father. Patrick Dawes." She expected shocked outcries but received only silence.

"Who is that?" Anne asked.

Catherine stared at her. "He robbed your father and caused him to commit suicide," she said slowly.

"I never heard of him," Anne said. "Who told you such a story?"

Catherine shook her head slowly. "I know my father well enough to know it's true. Lord Killian was—"

"My father?" Michael cried. "I should have known he'd have some hand in all this. Does he know that you and Edward were married?"

"I told him but he refuses to believe it," Catherine said. "That is why Simon married me. Your father had turned me from his door and I had nowhere to go."

"But Simon loves you!" Anne argued. "You can see it every time he looks at you."

243

"He certainly seems like a devoted husband to me," Michael agreed.

"It hardly matters now since I have to leave. If I do not, the whole scandal about my father will be brought out into the open."

"Why should it?" Michael asked. "We had never even heard of him, so who would be likely to connect you with him?"

There were only so many illusions she could destroy in one day. Catherine bit her lip and looked down at Teddy, saying nothing.

Michael understood though. "I see," he said in disgust. "My father will be happy to spread the news. But why?"

"Because of Teddy," Catherine said.

Michael looked bewildered for only a moment. "Of course, Teddy!"

Anne looked impatient. "I do not understand," she complained.

"Teddy is Edward's son," Michael said. "And his heir, and I assume Father does not like that idea."

Catherine nodded. "He does not believe that Edward would have chosen me to be the mother of the Killian children, he said. If I did not relinquish all claim to Edward's estate, he was going to tell about my father."

"Why, that devil!" Anne cried.

"That, my dear, is putting it a bit too nicely," Michael said dryly. "But can't you prove you and Edward were married?"

"I had marriage lines, but they are missing,"

244

Catherine admitted. "And it would take months to get another copy. By that time he will have ruined me and brought disgrace on the family. I thought it would be best if I just left."

"No, it would not," Anne declared, taking hold of Catherine's hand as if she would forcibly keep her there. "There must be something we can do." She looked at Michael hopefully.

Michael nodded grimly. "I think it's time to visit my father."

Madeline sipped her tea, then put her cup on the table before her. "I do not see why you are so upset," she told her father. "It really is rather funny."

Lord Killian glared at her, obviously unable to see the humor she saw.

"Does she really think she can outwit you?" Madeline laughed. "I will wager that she will be back here by tomorrow pleading for another chance to sign your paper."

"If she does, I shan't let her," he snapped. "It will be my great pleasure to see her ruined."

Madeline just smiled. "Would you like some more tea?" she offered. As she refilled his cup a commotion was heard from the hallway.

"What the devil!" Lord Killian shouted, jumping to his feet. A moment later Simon burst into the room, followed closely by Nigel. "What is the meaning of this outrageous intrusion?"

"I would like to know where my wife is," Simon

demanded.

"How the devil would I know where your wife is?"

Nigel pushed himself in front of Simon. "You must excuse Simon, my lord. He is understandably distraught at his wife's disappearance." Lord Killian frowned as Nigel turned to Madeline. "Have you any idea where she might have gone?" he asked her.

Madeline rose to her feet slowly and went to her father's side. Why was Nigel getting involved in all this? "I have no idea where she is, but I cannot say that I am terribly concerned," Madeline said. "After the terrible way she tried to use Edward's death, she does not deserve much concern."

Simon glared at her. "What are you talking about 'using Edward's death'? She was married to your brother. She had a right to expect some help from his family."

"She had a right to nothing!" Lord Killian declared.

Simon started forward, but Nigel grabbed his arm.

Madeline wasn't worried though. She and her father were in the right and that was all that mattered. "If she was married to Edward, as you claim," Madeline asked them, "why would she leave rather than admit it? Or is it possible that she was afraid the truth would come out?"

"I do not know why she left," Simon snapped. "But it was not because of Edward. I have the feeling, though, that someone here knows more about this than he is telling." Simon glared at Lord Killian.

"This is getting us nowhere," Nigel interrupted while keeping ahold of Simon's arm. His voice was calm but surprisingly authoritative. "Do either of you have any idea where Catherine might have gone?"

Madeline watched in astonishment as both men shook their heads, still angry, but no longer about to lock horns. More noise was heard from the hallway.

"Now what?" Lord Killian said, and striding over to the door pulled it open. Michael stood in the doorway. Close behind him were Anne and Catherine.

"Catherine!" Simon cried in relief. He hurried over to the doorway and pulled her forward into his arms. "Where have you been?"

Madeline turned away from the display. Catherine didn't deserve such love, not when she tried to hurt them all so. Still, her eyes went back to Simon and saw the cherishing way he held his wife. The sight awakened a strange longing in her heart that confused her, so she turned slightly to watch Michael and Anne come into the room also. Michael closed the door. "And to what do I owe the honor of this visit?" Lord Killian wondered aloud as he glared at them all.

"Merely that I take exception to your refusal to recognize Edward's son and heir," Michael said firmly.

Madeline shook off her strange moodiness and

laughed. She had to be strong for Edward's sake, for her father's. "His heir!" she said. "An heir must be born in wedlock, not out of it."

Simon's arm tightened around Catherine's shoulders. "Teddy is Edward's legal son," Catherine insisted. "We were married."

"And do you have proof?" Madeline asked with a faint smile.

"Of course she does," Simon said, and looked down at Catherine. "Where are . . ."

She just sighed and shook her head. "They are gone."

"How convenient," scoffed Lord Killian.

"No, how strange," Michael interjected. Madeline found his eyes on her, hard and accusing. "How could they have disappeared from Catherine's possession?"

Madeline just looked from Michael to Simon to Nigel, but found no softness, no understanding in any of their eyes.

"That is an excellent question," Nigel nodded. "Is it not strange that a thief would take only a piece of paper?"

"All of these questions are ridiculous, for that paper was worthless," Lord Killian said impatiently. "It was an obvious forgery."

Why were they all staring at her as if she were the one doing wrong, not Catherine? She had to make them see the light. "Besides," Madeline said quickly, "we have other proof that Edward did not marry her."

248

Catherine frowned. "What proof?" she demanded.

"Edward himself said so," Madeline said, turning to her father quickly. "Show them the letters from Edward you told me about. You kept all his things. You must still have them."

But Lord Killian only shrugged his shoulders. "I do not have to show them personal letters from my son," he said.

"But then they'll—"

Her father's frown deepened, the flash of anger in his eyes was directed at Madeline now. "It is her burden to prove they were married."

Madeline shook her head slowly. Why wouldn't he show them? Certainly the letters were personal and private, but showing them would end these awful accusing stares. "Yes, of course it is, but—"

"Maybe there are no letters, Madeline," Michael said.

"No." She spun around angrily to glare at the others. The anger in their eyes had softened into pity, and that made her rage burn even higher. "No! Father told me about the letters. They exist." She looked to her father, her eyes begging him to prove that they were right.

But her father's gaze had turned cold. "What is all this fuss about letters or no letters? Isn't Edward the important issue right now?" he said. "We have to keep his memory pure."

"I would say Teddy is the important issue," Simon noted.

"But wait!" Catherine interrupted them all suddenly with a happy cry. They all turned to stare at her. "There is other proof. I just remembered that it was in my Bible. It is in my bag."

"That is hardly proof," Lord Killian sneered, but Michael had hurried out to the hallway. He brought a scruffy-looking carpetbag back in to her while Anne took Teddy from her arms.

It took Catherine only a moment to find what she was looking for. "Here it is," she said with a smile, and held the book open to the family record. "Edward even wrote it in himself."

"Let me see that," Lord Killian cried, striding across the room in large steps. He glanced quickly down at the page, then again. "That is not his handwriting."

Catherine's face lost some of its glow. "It is," she insisted.

"I am certain that someone else could identify his writing," Nigel pointed out, looking directly at Madeline.

Simon's eyes reflected his astonishment. She could tell that he couldn't believe that Nigel would ask her to look at the Bible. He was certain that she would just agree with her father, regardless of the truth. But the truth was exactly what she wanted to convince the others of.

With her head held high, Madeline walked over to where Catherine stood. She took the book in her hands and looked down at the page. The first notice was about Catherine's parents, and she skipped

250

down to the next one.

Edward James Corbett-Smith married Catherine Ellen Dawes on Tuesday, March 12, 1812.

She read it once, then read it again, more slowly, her eyes tracing the cramped, angular style that was uniquely Edward's. How many times had she seen it in copy books and in letters? She frowned and looked up at her father. How hadn't he recognized it?

Lord Killian met her eyes. The coldness in his gaze ordered her to deny that it was Edward's handwriting. Why would he want her to do that? She stared down at the book again.

She could not understand why her beloved brother would marry such a nobody as Catherine, but it certainly seemed to be true. He would hardly have written it in the Bible if it were not.

"Well, Madeline," Nigel prompted. She looked up at him, biting her lower lip nervously. Simon sighed impatiently, expecting her denial.

Suddenly Madeline saw Teddy in Anne's arms. If Edward had been married to Catherine, then that was his son! That little baby was all they had left of Edward. How could her father turn him away? They should cherish him as they had Edward.

"It is Edward's writing," she said quietly, and pushed the book back into Catherine's hands.

A sigh of relief went up around the room, and Catherine threw her arms around Simon, but Madeline barely noticed. She was looking across at her father, but his eyes were unforgiving.

"Father," she said tentatively. Lord Killian turned away.

"Since Teddy has been acknowledged as Edward's son and heir, it would hardly help Edward's memory if it were known that he had married Patrick Dawes's daughter. Correct, Father?" Michael asked coldly.

Lord Killian stood unmoving for a long moment, then he nodded.

"I think it is time that we went home, then," Nigel said.

Madeline felt his touch on her arm, but she couldn't turn. "Please, Father," she said to his back. "Please, you have to understand. I loved Edward, and the baby is all we have of him now." But her father refused to turn around. She sighed and allowed Nigel to lead her toward the door.

Catherine stopped her, putting her hand gently on her arm. "I want to thank you for what you did," she said.

Madeline just stared at her. Some of the anger she had felt slipped away, and she turned slightly to look at Teddy as Anne gave him back to Catherine. Madeline watched him silently, then reached out her hand to gently stroke his cheek. He smiled at her and she smiled back.

"Is his name really Edward?" she asked Catherine.

Catherine nodded. "Would you rather we went by that name?"

Madeline was surprised at the question. "Oh,

yes," she admitted after a moment. "I would like that."

Nigel squeezed her arm slightly and she walked out with him. Her father did not move as they all left the room. Just before a footman closed the doors, Madeline glanced back. He was still standing rigidly straight, his back to the door. He would never forgive her, she realized. She had tried to give him everything and ended up alone.

Nigel handed her her bonnet and reticule, then took them back to carry them himself when she seemed not to know what to do with them. No, not alone, she suddenly realized.

... ...

... ...

Epilogue

The sun was setting just beyond the line of trees, casting a golden glow over the world that the autumn leaves reflected even in the shadows. Catherine leaned on the balcony railing, feeling the peace and serenity of Bradleigh surround her. Something else surrounded her just then—Simon's arms—and she turned to smile at him.

"Happy?" he asked.

"Only ecstatically so."

"You don't miss the excitement of the season?"

"I thought things were pretty exciting around here lately."

His smile deepened as he pulled her closer into his embrace. "I have a feeling they're going to get even more exciting next spring."

Catherine lay in his arms, a smile on her lips and a glow in her heart. It was too early to feel the baby move inside her, but her heart was so overflowing with love that she almost could. "I think little Edward is going to like having a brother or sister."

"It'll be exciting news to tell Anne and Michael when they get back from Italy."

"Between us, and then Nigel and Madeline expecting a baby also, the family is suddenly growing by leaps and bounds."

"I feel like a prosperous old country gentleman at the prospect of all these children running around the estate."

Catherine smiled in her heart and snuggled deeper into his arms. "You know what I feel? Unbelievably lucky."

"No. I'm the lucky one," Simon corrected her, brushing the top of her hair with his lips. "No more lingering worries about your father or Edward?"

She shook her head. "I had no control over my father's actions years ago, and Edward, well, I just feel sorry for him now. He wasn't a very happy person, and I don't think he would have ever been if he had lived."

"How can you be so generous?" Simon asked. "If he came up the walk now, I'd horsewhip him, just for starters."

Catherine laughed and turned in his arms to stare out at the setting sun once more. "Just look at that," she said, waving her arm over the golden expanse. "Peaceful surroundings and a loving family. What more does anyone need from life? What good would it do to harbor hatred and block peace from entering your soul? No matter what Edward did or meant to do, I am wonderfully happy now. In fact, I'm actually grateful to him."

"Grateful to that worthless scoundrel?" Simon's

voice echoed his astonishment.

Catherine smiled at him. "Just think if he had told his family about me and they accepted my and the baby's presence, then I never would have gone back to that inn and never had the chance to rescue you from the dregs of depravity you were trying to drink yourself into."

"I was not drunk," Simon pointed out with a teasing laugh. "But I am now, without brandy even. I just need a smile from you and I'm foxed beyond belief."

"Sounds dangerous, this power I have."

"Oh, it is." He slipped his arm over her shoulder. "What do you say we go inside and explore just how dangerous it is?"

"With pleasure, my dear husband."